Michael Levitt is a practising surgeon and hospital administrator. He grew up, was educated and continues to live and work in Perth, Western Australia. He is married and has three adult children and three grandchildren.

Michael has been an avid art collector for many years and has written numerous pieces for magazines, newspapers and exhibition catalogues. He is the author of three books dealing with health non-fiction and published his first work of fiction, The Gallerist, in 2022. In January 2023, he was awarded an AM for services to medical administration and to Australian professional bodies.

Michael Levitt

THE MASKED BALL

AUSTIN MACAULEY PUBLISHERS™
LONDON * CAMBRIDGE * NEW YORK * SHARJAH

Copyright © Michael Levitt 2024

The right of Michael Levitt to be identified as author of this work has been asserted by the author in accordance with sections 77 and 78 of the Copyright, Designs and Patents Act 1988.

All rights reserved. No part of this publication may be reproduced, stored in a retrieval system, or transmitted in any form or by any means, electronic, mechanical, photocopying, recording, or otherwise, without the prior permission of the publishers.

Any person who commits any unauthorised act in relation to this publication may be liable to criminal prosecution and civil claims for damages.

This is a work of fiction. Names, characters, businesses, places, events, locales, and incidents are either the products of the author's imagination or used in a fictitious manner. Any resemblance to actual persons, living or dead, or actual events is purely coincidental.

A CIP catalogue record for this title is available from the British Library.

ISBN 9781035843022 (Paperback)
ISBN 9781035843039 (ePub e-book)

www.austinmacauley.com

First Published 2024
Austin Macauley Publishers Ltd®
1 Canada Square
Canary Wharf
London
E14 5AA

"Art is the whisper of history …"

Julian Barnes, 2016 in *The Noise of Time*

He staggered down the footpath as if blinded by his panic. It was a still, cool winter night but the horror of the last few hours had heightened the anxiety he experienced whenever he'd been doing cocaine, and he was drenched in perspiration. He lurched into the side-street in which three hours earlier, unfamiliar with his surroundings, he'd jagged a parking spot.

Reflexively, he felt his pockets, front and back, for cigarettes, in need of something to quell the chaos in his head. But all that was there were his car keys.

A loud explosion about one hundred metres away made him jump, jolting his thoughts back into focus. He pressed the remote, and the nearby flash of his car's headlights drew him towards it. He lowered his tall frame into the car and turned on the ignition, the sound of the engine muffling the first distant shouts of alarm.

He wiped the sweat off his face and neck using a towel lying on the front passenger seat, soiled from his last visit to the gym. He gripped the steering wheel tightly with both hands, taking deep, slow breaths, willing himself to calm down. He had followed the instructions he'd been given to the letter, and knew that he had to get moving, that there was no time now for him to dwell on what had just taken place. He drove off, heading away from the mayhem as steadily as his nerves would allow, the rising wail of whining sirens descending upon the inferno he'd created like a swarm of enraged wasps.

Blasts of fear and self-loathing discharged in his head as he wended his way towards safer territory, unable to banish a terrifying apparition of fiery death.

Chapter 1
Sunday, 19 August 1934

Rachel descended from the bus into the hazy Sunday sunlight and tried to gain her bearings. She had alighted at the first stop on Rudolph Road, the trip from Chelsea requiring two buses and taking more than half an hour, unimaginable to her for such a short distance, especially on a weekend. The weather had been warm and uncomfortable since she'd arrived in London almost three weeks earlier, but today it was outright oppressive. She continued up Rudolph on foot and crossed the road when the traffic allowed. The first right was Oxford Road and she looked for number 37, about half a dozen houses from the corner, on her right.

The flowers she had brought with her from a stall just outside her Chelsea flat were already wilting and her hair, uncut since she sailed from Melbourne in June, was plastered by perspiration to her forehead and, as always, subservient to the widow's peak that had dogged her for her entire life. She regretted not taking the time to have her hair cut before meeting up with the Brodzkys.

Rachel arrived at the address to which Bob had directed her – a three-storey, semi-detached house that, she observed, resembled more or less every other house along the street; and that resembled more or less every other street she had encountered in London so far. London, she'd found, was at once familiar and foreign. It was Sunday and Oxford Road was deserted, its residents vanquished, she imagined, by the protracted heatwave.

She knocked on the door. She had met Alfred Brodney, known as Bob, in Melbourne. It was his older brother, Horace Brodzky, the artist—who had retained the family name—and Horace's wife Bertha who she was visiting. Ex-pats with whom to connect, perhaps, while she was in London. She did not have their telephone number and, as the wait for a response to her knocking grew longer, she wished she had written to them in advance to forewarn them of her visit. Granted, in this weather, the family might have gone out in search of some relief. The thought of having made a futile excursion in such cruel conditions was flattening.

Rachel knocked again. This time, she heard a child calling out from inside the house and the sound of footsteps approaching the front door. She swept her hair off her forehead and cradled the flowers in front of her, willing them back to life. The door opened.

"Hello?"

He was gaunt, older than Bob, a little worn-out, she thought. He had black hair receding at his temples, a straight, black moustache in the English style, and a stern gaze; the familial resemblance was clear. His grey trousers were held up by suspenders over an off-white singlet.

"Hello. My name is Rachel Blazov. I'm here from Australia," she said, suddenly self-conscious about her accent. "You'll be Horace, am I right?"

She saw him inspect her, then her flowers, conscious of the bedraggled appearance she shared with them, hoping that his wife would soon appear to rescue her.

"Yes, that's me. You must be a friend of my brother's."

"Yes," Rachel said with relief. "We're … friends," she hesitated, unsure in that instant of Horace's political views, "from the communist party in Melbourne. And he gave me your address when I told him I was coming to London to work. I've just started at the Royal Brompton. I'm a physiotherapist. I hope I'm not intruding."

Brodzky said nothing.

"Here. I've brought these for Mrs Brodzky," and she stretched out both hands towards him.

Horace's gaze turned to a frown, his eyes sad. "Well, you see, Mrs Brodzky has recently returned to New York. For good, I mean. Come on—you'd better come in out of the heat. You look like you could do with a cold drink. But I'm afraid those flowers have passed the point of no return. And what good are flowers, anyway? You can't eat them."

Chapter 2
Wednesday, 11 January 2023

Aresh Mehta looked around his North Adelaide apartment living room, its emptiness meeting with his approval yet still triggering a brief shiver of anxiety. This was only one of many moves he had made in his life so far and, he could well imagine, not necessarily the last. Moving to Perth, to take up a full-time position as a gynaecological oncologist at King Edward Memorial Hospital, well known across the country not least for its reputedly contentious culture, carried with it pangs of uncertainty. He would have to settle once again into an unfamiliar environment and, after many years of fleeting attachments to a variety of workplaces, there was now the distinct threat of permanence. And with that thought, in particular, a tremble of claustrophobia reverberated through his body.

The handful of boxes packed with the belongings he intended to keep had been removed the day before. Every single piece of furniture—table lamps, posters, vases and other trinkets—accumulated over the last three years of his training in Adelaide and of little value or lasting meaning to him, had just been taken, with glee and disbelief, by the first person to answer his advertisement on Marketplace.

One thing, however, he could not sell or leave behind was Lisa's painting. Or whoever's painting it had been. It had been left outside the door of his Coogee apartment in Sydney—which he'd shared with Lisa and another housemate—just after Lisa had left for a weekend, joining her family for a holiday on the New South Wales Central Coast. Aresh had found it, wrapped and propped against the wall beside the front door of their second-floor unit, when he returned to the empty apartment late one Friday evening. He'd just worked a full day at Sydney Women's Hospital, right at the start of his journey towards specialist qualification.

The painting had a post-it note with nothing more than "Lisa" written on it. Lisa had only recently moved to Sydney from Newcastle to be closer to her on-again, off-again boyfriend, a pharmacist at nearby Prince of Wales Hospital. Aresh had taken the painting in and had placed it on Lisa's bed in her room.

That weekend holiday with her family turned out to be a sort of "French exit" for Lisa. She'd texted her flatmates on the Sunday evening to let them know that she wasn't returning and that her relationship with the pharmacist was over "for good". Her aunt, who lived nearby, would be coming to collect her belongings sometime in the next week and Lisa would be changing her phone number and blocking all social media access. She'd paid her rent one month in advance and that SMS, she made clear, would be the last they'd hear from her.

The painting stood in Lisa's room all week waiting for her aunt to collect it. Aresh could still remember the way its presence had played on his mind and the strength of the urge he'd felt to unwrap it and have a look. By the Thursday, with no sign of Lisa's aunt, he'd relented and inspected it. It was painted on a canvas that, he'd subsequently measured, was sixty centimetres square.

It was a grim scene, rendered in clear detail, set in an elegant private study of sorts, bookshelves in dark wood, ornaments mingling with the books, a HiFi system and an old-fashioned floor lamp. The brushstrokes were precise, deft use of light and shade highlighting two human figures. A young woman, looking directly at the viewer, was spreadeagled—prone, her clothing torn—over the large office desk where it appeared that she was being sexually assaulted by a tall male figure, his own shirt ripped open to expose his chest and abdomen. He had a black mask that partly obscured his face, although his shock of dark hair and the menace in his grin were unmistakeable.

The mask that the presumed rapist wore was mirrored by masks being worn by characters in a small painting the artist had depicted hanging on one of the study's walls, situated in the upper left of the painting. A sort of painting within a painting. Aresh also noted a prominent vertical upper abdominal scar on the male figure indicating prior abdominal surgery, unusual in its location to the left of midline. It was a remarkable and very intimate detail to have included.

The young woman's sharply depicted features, her short hair, piercing blue eyes, perfectly shaped nose and pretty face, were almost as unsettling as the scene itself. Pain and anger, mixed with defiance, were apparent in her expression. She supported herself on her elbows, her left forearm on the desk, her left palm facing downwards. Her right arm was flexed at the elbow, her right forearm lifted off the desk and her index finger pointing almost casually back over her left shoulder towards her assailant.

The impression of reality—violent and sexual, but in no way salacious—was arresting. The painting was unsigned and Aresh had turned it over to see if the artist was identified on its reverse side. All that was written was: "Rape on the hill 19.1.2010". It wasn't clear to Aresh if that was the date the painting had been completed or the date of the incident it portrayed.

Disturbed but moved by the image, Aresh had re-wrapped the painting and put it back on the floor of Lisa's room, leaving it for collection presumably over the coming weekend when he was, once again, on duty. When he dragged himself back into his apartment the following Monday afternoon, a little shell-shocked after a punishing weekend of ward calls and having assisted at numerous operations and deliveries, he found that Lisa's room had finally been cleaned out. Except for the painting, which remained exactly where he had left it. It had not been claimed. The post-it note lay forsaken, upside down on the floor behind the painting.

True to her word, Lisa proved to be uncontactable. And, as things had turned out, just a fortnight later, Aresh also moved out of the Coogee apartment. His two-year-long relationship with his girlfriend, Zoe, had been on thin ice for some time, his reluctance to progress their relationship and his open diffidence about ever starting a family causing ever-increasing friction between them. The painting seemed somehow to be the final straw, Zoe disturbed and offended by the image, angry at Aresh for his lack of emotional commitment.

A position as a Service Registrar in Obstetrics and Gynaecology at Wodonga Hospital, where he had worked as an Intern, had turned up unexpectedly at that time. It was only a three-month contract, but Aresh thought it might be a useful steppingstone to a formal College-approved training programme. His underlying crisis of commitment and the humiliation he felt at being left by Zoe made the decision to move hospital, at very short notice, straightforward. He resigned from the Sydney Women's Hospital effective immediately.

Chapter 3
29 September 1884

David walked gingerly along the uneven path heading away from the port. It was cloudy and his threadbare clothing offered little resistance even to the gentle wind that blew off the bay. He was weak and gaunt, unkempt and sunburnt and he looked and felt much older than twenty-one years of age.

He had left his hometown of Blazowa in Galicia, southern Poland, two and a half years earlier—in defiance of his family—heading west across Poland without any clear plan. He'd been determined to escape what he believed was inevitable violence, as well as his family's suffocating expectations. Jews across Poland had been rocked by recent massacres in Warsaw and elsewhere in his country; his grandfather and uncle were esteemed rabbinic scholars into which lifestyle, if not the precise career, he knew he was destined to be enveloped. To David Spira, his future appeared to have been mapped out for him, unpredictable and perilous on the one hand, predestined and suffocating on the other. As far as he was concerned, there had been no other option for him but to leave.

He first travelled through Krakow, followed by a long trek, north-west towards Gdansk on the German coast. Over a period of almost six months, he experienced repeated violence and periods of hunger, and he had learnt to first hide and then deny his faith. He arrived at the coast convinced there was no safe future for him anywhere in his own country. When Germany proved no more welcoming, he joined the crew of a ship sailing to England.

Arriving at Harwich, on England's east coast, David soon made his way south towards London. Whereas the countryside was lush and green, he found London to be crowded, grey and unfriendly. Fearful of antisemitic sentiment, he maintained a neutral identity. Nevertheless, he gravitated to the city's East End where he felt most comfortable in the midst of its visibly Jewish population and numerous Polish-run businesses; he held down a succession of jobs and was able to afford board in a Polish household close to London Fields.

Life was good for well over a year. His Polish accent made it difficult for David to make himself understood, but he was quick to comprehend English. There was, however, no margin for error for foreigners. A good-humoured night out with fellow immigrants turned into a brawl to which the police were called; although he was only jailed overnight, his heritage was exposed and, without pity, his board and employment were terminated. Despite receiving assistance from the local Jewish community, David recognised the familiar themes of marginalisation and insecurity. Angry and as impulsive as ever, he chose to leave England.

The only ship on which he could find work was sailing to Australia. He had not appreciated that it would take almost three arduous months aboard the *Harbinger*, interrupted by dysentery, hunger and exposure to the elements, to reach his destination. It was now late September. To David, Melbourne port seemed orderly notwithstanding the throng of people and the buzz of activity. He was already in possession of his Australian papers, albeit with a novel surname, an abbreviation of his hometown in Poland, bestowed by the confused, impatient officials.

In this manner, David Spira—descendant of the Rebbe of Dinov, close kin of the illustrious Bluzhever Rebbe—commenced his new life in Australia as David Blazov. He was weak and wary of his new surroundings, but Melbourne would be his home for the rest of his life.

Chapter 4
Saturday, 13 May 2023

Aresh was still adapting to his life's latest iteration in Perth. Inside his new hospital's cultural bubble, he was more comfortable than he had anticipated. There was plenty of work for him to do, the oncology service was a skilled one, and he felt that his colleagues across the hospital appreciated the additional resource his arrival had brought to their combined services. He had bought a town house in Leederville, in a street lined on opposite sides by jacarandas and flame trees which, he'd been assured, would make it a scene of great beauty come late autumn and spring. His new home stood in clear line of sight of a grand old convent that towered over the entire suburb, now the headquarters of Catholic Education in Western Australia.

Yet, at thirty-six years of age, after a succession of moves around the country and now, quite remote from his Sydney family, Aresh's solitary lifestyle was beginning to hover over him like an intrusive drone. He hung *Rape on the Hill* in his new study and, as he had done for more than a decade, made sure that visitors did not get to see it. While he appreciated that the subject matter could be confronting to the unprepared eye, he had become transfixed by its technical brilliance and compelled by the story it seemed to tell.

He had long wondered who the artist was and what had motivated them to paint such a distressing scene. He had been unable to locate similar works online that might point to the artist's identity, having paid particular attention to a host of Sydney gallery websites. He'd tracked the activities of a number of current Australian artists who painted in a similar style, a style for which he had begun to develop an appreciation, without gaining even the vaguest clue as to who the artist might be. Despite all of the unknowns, Aresh had reached the confident conclusion that this was not some hidden masterpiece, that the artist was no one notable in the current Australian art scene.

A colleague at King Edward had mentioned the display of portrait paintings from the latest Lester Prize exhibition on show at the celebrated local private hospital, St John of God Subiaco. Aresh had only recently been to that hospital, to assist a colleague at an especially difficult case, and decided to take advantage of his weekend off-duty to walk the short distance from his home to the hospital and see the exhibition. He entered the building off McCourt Street and wandered through the well-lit main corridor, noting the names of the various specialists, none of them familiar, whose offices lined either side of the passage.

At a sort of intersection of corridors, a stairwell to his right, more offices ahead and, as signposted, the radiology department and main hospital to the left, he found the display of portraits about which he'd been told. A few other people were also looking at them. Aresh wasn't sure if they were patients, visitors of patients or, like him, people who'd come just to see the exhibition. As he explored the exhibition, he noted that the curator had grouped the works according to style, the more abstract pieces aggregated along the long corridor outside the radiology department, the realist pieces positioned in a wider, better lit space around a stairwell leading up to a second level of clinic offices.

"Hi Aresh. Are you a fan of portrait painting?"

Aresh turned sharply, caught by surprise by the approach. At first, he didn't recognise the woman speaking to him, adding to his discomfort. He was hopeless at faces.

"Hi! How are you? Yes, I was told that this was worth looking at. It's great. What do you think?"

She smiled. "I'm Cathy Nankervis, one of the anaesthetic registrars at King Eddie's. You probably don't recognise me without a cap and mask on."

"I'm sorry, Cathy, I really am bad at names. And faces. Thanks for helping me out."

"Don't apologise. Enjoy the paintings. It's nice to see you." She turned to head away.

"No, Cathy, don't go. I love looking at paintings. It'd be even better to look at them with you. Have you got time?"

Aresh spent the next hour with Cathy taking a leisurely look at the exhibition. He preferred the realist works, Cathy the more abstract ones; they both agreed the winner was a worthy painting. They continued their discussions about their shared appreciation of art over coffee at the hospital's in-house café situated closer to the main entrance.

"You know, I've got this one particular painting that I've had for more than a decade, that I … think is really excellent." Aresh smiled, hesitating for an instant about the wisdom of proceeding. "Something tells me it's by a really good artist. But I can't figure out who. To be honest, I don't even know if the artist is a man or a woman. I suspect I'll never find out who painted it. Or why."

"I'll be no use to you at all. I've only just begun to get interested in art, since I started at King Eddie's, actually."

Aresh searched Cathy's face, trying to discern her thoughts. "It's a pretty tough painting to look at," he added.

"One of my bosses, Derek Cummins—you know him—is a keen collector," Cathy continued, "and he's sparked my curiosity. Maybe we, I mean, you could ask him?" Cathy blushed.

"No, let's do that together. I've worked with Derek on a few emergencies. I'll speak to him on Monday."

Chapter 5
Tuesday, 16 May 2023

"Beaufort Gallery, Olivia speaking."

"Hi, Olivia. My name is Derek Cummins. I'm an anaesthetist and a colleague of Dr Lewis."

Olivia tensed slightly at the use of that title. Her father hadn't worked as a doctor for over five years, ever since establishing his art gallery and walking away from a thirty-year-long career as a surgeon. "How can I help you, Dr Cummins?"

"Please. Call me Derek. I'd really like to speak to Dr Lewis … to Mark, if I could. I'm keen to introduce him to a colleague who has a painting he'd like to find out more about."

"That shouldn't be a problem. I'm sure Mark would love to speak to you, and I know he'll be keen to help your friend sort out that painting, if he can. Would you like to speak to him, or should I just arrange a time for someone to bring the painting in for him to look at?"

Derek agreed that it made more sense to bring the painting in to be assessed in person and they agreed on a time for the following Saturday afternoon. They concluded the conversation and Olivia smiled to herself. She shared her father's intrigue at the origins of paintings. Maybe this would turn out to be that elusive hidden treasure about which he obsessed? Regardless, she hoped—for everyone's sake—it would not prove too difficult to resolve. Her father could be more than just a little obsessional when it came to art.

Chapter 6
Saturday, 20 May 2023

The three medicos descended on Beaufort Gallery after lunchtime. Mark Lewis greeted each of them with equal enthusiasm, always comfortable in the company of his former colleagues so many of whom, he knew, felt a strong connection to, and affection for, art. The gallery was otherwise empty of visitors, the fine late autumn day having lured people elsewhere.

Aresh unwrapped the painting and Mark placed it on an easel. He stepped back and inspected it, chin on hand. The entourage held its collective breath.

Mark then approached the painting, turned it around, a transient grimace betraying his momentary distaste. Replacing the painting on the easel, he looked at it again with evident concern. He peered closely at the male figure, the woman's face, and the small painting in the upper left corner of the work. He walked to his desk and withdrew a magnifying glass from its top drawer.

He went back to the painting and examined under magnification the small group of masked figures depicted in that little painting. Nodding, he turned to speak to the group.

"Well. This is an incredible piece of painting, that's for sure. I don't recognise the artist although I think I probably should. It's technically brilliant and the scene it depicts seems totally believable. Where did you get this from?"

Aresh spoke up. "It's mine, I suppose. I've had it for more than ten years. It was sort of delivered, out of the blue, to the apartment I was sharing with a few other people, in Sydney. The person it was meant for had just moved out for good and never came back to claim it. I took it with me when I left a little while later and I have to admit that I've long since stopped trying to return it." He glanced at Cathy. "I didn't expect anyone would want it back anyway. It's a bit grim, to be honest, and it's probably contributed to the end of a few of my relationships.

But I can't bring myself get rid of it." Aresh looked at his feet and added in a small voice. "I'm sort of hooked on it."

Mark smiled. He could well relate to that sort of irrational attachment to a work of art.

"What caught your eye in that little painting on the study wall?" asked Derek.

"Yes, that is very intriguing. I don't recognise the work, but it has been painted in considerable detail. The artist has even gone to the trouble of signing and dating it by its own artist. But I suppose you've already seen that."

Aresh blushed. "I noted the masks and can see how the artist has also placed a mask on the rapist. I've never focused on that signature, though. I haven't looked at that bit quite so closely." He turned towards Cathy and shrugged.

"Well, that little painting within a painting has been signed 'H. Brodzky' and has been dated '34. I know of Horace Brodzky. He painted in the first half of the twentieth century, so that fits. But I really don't know enough off the top of my head to say much more about him. And the inclusion of that detail strikes me as important somehow."

"How so?" asked Cathy.

"I'm not exactly sure" replied Mark. "The artist has reproduced Brodzky's figurative style in the main part of the painting. And the villain is masked just like the characters in the small painting, as Aresh says. Perhaps, the artist wanted to pay homage to Brodzky by emulating his style in this work?"

"Or they'd seen exactly this painting by Brodzky somewhere and they wanted to acknowledge it specifically?" asked Derek.

Mark looked closely at the entire work once again. "If that is an attempt to represent an original Brodzky, you're right, the artist might be identifying a real scene. Maybe this is a real office, and this was a painting hanging there? Maybe it's a statement about male behaviour in general or possibly even about the character depicted?" Mark suppressed a wry smile – throughout history, artists had sought to deliver hidden messages or, occasionally, make seditious political commentary through their paintings. Perhaps this artist was weaving their own story through these characters and objects.

"Maybe this is a real event taking place in a real location," Aresh said. "It has always felt very real to me. That would be potentially …. quite serious."

"There is also that abdominal scar," said Derek. "That seems distinctive, almost explicit. You were an abdominal surgeon, Mark, does that incision look credible to you?"

"Possibly. Judging by that thick head of hair, I'd say the assailant is a younger man, maybe in his mid-thirties or forty at the most. A left paramedian incision is a bit old-fashioned. Let's say this painting was from 2010 as the date indicates. Maybe he'd had the operation as a teenager, at the very earliest, say, around 1990. Probably later. Laparoscopic surgery for General Surgeons really only got started in Australia back in about 1990. Most major abdominal operations were performed using long incisions until well into the new millennium. And a left upper quadrant incision in a young man? Maybe gastric surgery, a perforated ulcer. A splenectomy for ITP? Maybe for trauma. It wasn't a common incision even then."

The group of four were silent for a moment as they pondered what message the painting conveyed. Mark broke the silence. "We have some work to do. I have to find out more about Brodzky and see if that little painting at least is known to anyone. Aresh, you should contact your old roommate. He'll probably know the artist."

"It was a girl, actually. The roommate. Her name was Lisa. I don't remember her surname, or what she did." Aresh appeared a little shame-faced. "I don't really know what happened to her."

"You didn't know your roommate's name?" asked Cathy with an incredulous expression.

"Yes, well, she only moved in with her boyfriend about a month before she more or less disappeared," Aresh said, sounding a little defensive. He thought for a moment. "Maybe it was a bit longer."

"I suppose you could try to contact her boyfriend. You did know *his* name, didn't you?" asked Cathy, smiling.

"I did know it back then. But that was more than a decade ago. He was a pharmacist at one of the other hospitals in that part of Sydney. I'll try to dig that up. It was Gerry or Jeremy or …. I remember Lisa's name because I've kept the post-it note with her name on it."

"You kept the post-it note?"

Aresh stared at Cathy as if pleading with her to give him some space. "It wasn't really my painting."

"OK, Aresh," Mark interrupted, "see if you can track down Lisa or her ex. I'd really like to hold on to the painting, if you don't mind. There's someone I know whose opinion might be very helpful."

Aresh exhaled. "OK. Yes. I suppose that's alright. I haven't been apart from this painting for a very long time." He smiled, "It'll be OK."

Cathy shook her head.

"While we're here" said Derek, "do you mind if we have a look around?"

Chapter 7
Wednesday, 24 May 2023

Elizabeth Green assumed her regular seat at The Lookout café overlooking Rushcutters Bay. She was, as usual, ten minutes early for her weekly catch-up with her girlfriends, a group of six loyal friends united by decades of competitive socialising and fundraising, high society snobbery and the shared appreciation of their good fortune. In every case, that good fortune had been built upon the wealth of the families into which they had married.

And Sam Green's family, into which Elizabeth had married, was one of them. He was now a resident at the Moran Nursing Home in Vaucluse. After more than two years of caring for him at home with his progressively deteriorating dementia, Elizabeth had become depressed, almost suicidal. No amount of home help could ease the distress of Sam's forgetfulness, paranoid outbursts and loss of simple social skills. Despite the inevitability of his placement in residential care, it had not been until he'd had a fall and a head injury, resulting in a chaotic trip to St Vincent's Hospital late one Saturday night, that they were separated. Sam had never made it home and his life was now very much in limbo, unable to communicate meaningfully and eking out a limited existence, shrouded by Elizabeth's self-reproachful anticipation of his inevitable demise.

She sipped on her coffee and breathed in the glorious view, grateful for her well-maintained health and cognition. Sam had been a wonderful husband, attentive and supportive. They had both grown up in Melbourne, where they met in their mid-twenties. He was tall, handsome, clever in business and already well to do. She had been beautiful, ambitious and controlling. She smiled to herself – they had been a perfect match.

Well, almost. Sam came from a traditional Jewish family who had not taken kindly to Elizabeth. Sam wasn't strongly attached to his religion but his attachment to his small family and wide circle of friends in Melbourne was powerful. She moved to Sydney—an expensive and risky gamble—to draw him away from the close-knit community that presented such intense competition for his loyalty. It worked and, lovesick, Sam had followed her and abandoned much of his former life.

That had, she believed, worked out well for them both. But their children had not been so lucky. Sarah, the oldest, named after Sam's grandmother, his father's late mother, lost in the Holocaust, had been spoiled and had rebelled. Her ill-considered marriage to a drug-addled musician had ended in predictable grief and protracted upheaval before, chastened and helpless, she had returned to her parents' home with her children in tow. Over the space of the last few years, Sarah and the children had recovered, recalibrated and moved on, very much accepting of Elizabeth's direction and financial support. Sarah had re-partnered, making an altogether more astute choice in men, and had moved out again. The children were now independent young adults.

Elizabeth's son, Bradley, had been a joy as a child, his easy-going nature and good looks serving him well. On the other hand, he had little of his father's self-discipline and even less of his mother's ambition. As a teenager, he flew under the radar while his parents were preoccupied with his wayward older sister. He was happy to feign interest in the family's ever-growing property development business but never involved himself in the detail. He'd remained a passive contributor at best and the company's senior executives had come to hold him in low regard, a likeable but indolent man.

Sam had adored his son—they both did—and they'd surrounded him with capable people who shielded him from having to make decisions of substance. In reality, he had little responsibility and even less influence in the running of the company that he had, in name, now come to control; and he never complained about either.

A large motorboat caught Elizabeth's eye, cruising across the harbour, heading east past Clark Island in the direction of Watson's Bay. She checked her wristwatch; her friends would be only minutes away.

Bradley had married a lovely woman who had borne her two more precious grandchildren and who had persevered through a series of Bradley's extra-marital affairs before admitting defeat and accepting a substantial divorce settlement. Elizabeth appreciated her good fortune in still having contact with

Brad's children, tall and good-looking like their father yet warm and capable like their mother.

Mercifully, Bradley had not sought to torture any other woman by marrying again, although he continued to turn up with new girlfriends at his side, younger and more gullible with every passing relationship. She knew that she would intervene on the girl's behalf if any serious consideration of marriage emerged. These girls deserved a better life than her son could possibly provide, regardless of his wealth.

Marianne Coates was the first to arrive, Elizabeth noting with real pleasure that her friend's elegant bearing had begun to return, now almost six months after her hip replacement. "Marianne, you're looking very well. Come and sit down."

Chapter 8
Monday, 22 May 2023

Eager to investigate the origins of Aresh's painting, Mark had arranged to meet his mentor Pat O'Beirne at Pat's Welshpool storeroom on Monday, the one day of the week Beaufort Gallery did not open. Mark had found an incongruously chic café and coffee roaster around the corner from the storeroom from which, én route, he had collected their morning drinks.

Upon entering, Mark was greeted by a magnificent Howard Taylor, hanging above the front reception desk where Aleyah, one of Pat and Helen's longstanding employees, was seated. "That's beautiful" Mark said.

"It's one of Randall's," said Aleyah. "We store it for him, and he wanted to have a look at it when he pops in later in the week." Randall Phillips was, Mark knew, a Perth barrister with a fine collection of art.

"Something else to fantasise about," Mark replied with a smile, heading through to Pat's office. He greeted Pat, placed the coffees on the table and headed back to his car, retrieving Aresh's painting, and carrying it back inside. Mark carefully took the painting off the easel that was facing Pat's desk. It was a work in oil, on canvas, that portrayed a solitary tree on a hillside in the Impressionist style. Mark noted that it was by Arthur Boyd and dated '1937', making it a work from Boyd's teenage years.

"That's in next week's sale," said Pat. "It's wonderful, isn't it?"

Mark nodded in agreement as he replaced the Boyd with Aresh's painting and turned to face Pat. "This work is dated January 2010. It's a confronting image but it isn't signed." Mark stepped away to allow Pat to inspect it. At that moment, Helen O'Beirne entered the office from its other door which opened onto their vast storeroom, packed with its ever-changing selection of wonders and delights. "I'm sorry, Helen. I didn't know you'd be here. I didn't bring you a coffee."

"Not a problem, Mark. I've had one already. How are you? And how're Linda and Olivia and all the family?"

Mark and Helen exchanged pleasantries while Pat examined the new painting. Soon, Helen's attention was also drawn to it, both of them using a magnifying glass, one after the other, to interrogate the little internal painting hanging on the study wall. The room was silent, all three gallerists absorbed in thought.

Pat looked away first, catching Mark's eye. "I've never seen *that* Brodzky. But it certainly looks like it could be one. That'll be Brodzky himself on the left. He occasionally painted himself in his own works."

"It is a little small and indistinct, but I really like that two-dimensional cast of characters," said Mark.

"Brodzky took that style from Piero Della Francesca, an Italian who painted in the sixteenth century. Della Francesca used flat groupings of people and distinctive hand gestures. You can see both those features in the little painting the artist has attributed to Brodzky. That makes me believe that it could be based on a real Brodzky."

"And they've replicated that style in the hand gesture of the victim. That finger pointing over her shoulder at her assailant," said Helen.

Mark nodded, absorbing anew the subtle detail of both paintings.

"Henry Lew might recognise that little work," Helen continued. "We've got a copy of his book about Brodzky, haven't we?"

"Do you know him?" asked Mark.

"Henry? Sure. He's a retired Ophthalmologist, in Melbourne I think," said Pat.

"And an author," Helen added. "Historical stuff, mainly. He's an expert on the entire Brodzky family."

Mark had heard of Lew and, in his quest for more information about Brodzky, had already located his book about Brodzky online. Mark wasn't surprised Helen and Pat had a copy. "It's only tiny," said Mark, pointing towards the group of four painted figures. "Do you think it's supposed to be a real Brodzky or just something in his style?"

"It really is difficult to be sure," said Pat slowly shaking his head. "I'm also struggling to understand the bigger narrative here. It's a shocking scene. I think the artist is trying to tell us something. I mean, a number of things seem to be pointing us towards the masked man's identity. If that little Brodzky is real, the bigger painting might depict a location that's also real. The attacker's hair is distinctive, almost a bit of a caricature, and that abdominal scar seems like a very specific feature to have included. It's as if the artist is trying to tell us who the attacker is and where this is all happening. But to what end?" Pat shrugged his shoulders and sat back on his desk.

Helen spoke up. "My take on it is that the artist is incriminating that masked man in a rape. Possibly in her own rape. That could be our artist right there." Helen gesticulated towards the victim. "Look at her. She's looking straight at us. She's speaking to us – 'He raped me, don't let him get away with it.' I'm not sure why she's used a painting to make that point, but it all looks mighty real to me."

There was an awkward silence. Pat started leafing through Lew's book, pointing out an illustration of a painting in which Brodzky had included himself. The English moustache and the receding hairline were a good match for the man depicted in miniature on the easel. "That little painting isn't reproduced in this book. And I've never seen it in circulation. If it is real, Henry Lew might know where it is. If he does know …" Pat fell silent.

Mark wondered what they'd do if they did locate the Brodzky. What would they ask of the owners? "I don't suppose this artist rings any bells with you?" Mark asked, pointing to the painting on the easel. "From the owner's story, it's almost certainly a Sydney artist."

Helen shook her head and looked at Pat. "Me neither, Mark" he said. "It's well-crafted and cleverly conceived. But that doesn't mean the artist is well known. If it was a real incident, you'd think she'd have also exposed her attacker in some other way, reported it to the police." All three of them stood still, thinking.

"Or maybe she thought it would be a matter of whose word the police would believe?" Helen added.

"What if she was in a relationship with him, and he assaulted her. Or rejected her. You know, upset her badly," said Pat.

"And she painted this to expose him" said Mark, the pieces seeming to fall into place. "People who knew him well would recognise him from that hair and from that abdominal scar. Or from the location, even if the attack took place elsewhere."

"Maybe that's why she gave the painting to someone else to hold on to for her," added Helen. "Perhaps she'd had second thoughts or felt it was too blatant an accusation?"

"Or else the painting was made in anger, or as some sort of social statement, and she's thought better of it" said Pat, his tone measured. "Who knows? It's possible there might have been a police investigation that's already been and gone. I don't think you can assume that this is an accurate portrayal of a real event just because it's been so well depicted."

"Maybe I should start with the Sydney police?" Mark looked at Helen, then Pat, and immediately sensed their alarm in the widening of their eyes. He smiled as reassuringly as he could. "Don't worry, I'll think about that for a bit before I get too involved."

Chapter 9
Saturday, 27 May 2023

The rain reminded Aresh of Sydney, bucketing down like a waterfall. He had invited Cathy out for dinner, her six-month term at King Edward having ended early courtesy of her taking accumulated annual and study leave in the lead-up to her final anaesthesia examinations. He hoped he was not transgressing any boundaries; she was, in any event, older than most of her fellow Trainees having worked, she'd told him, as a General Practitioner for a few years before deciding to pursue a different career direction.

Even still, Aresh was a little on edge at the potential repercussions of dating a junior colleague just a few months after starting at a new hospital. He didn't feel predatory in his motives or his actions, but who knew precisely how this might be construed? He hoped that, on this date at least, they would not bump into anyone either of them knew.

He saw her enter off St George's Terrace, having removed her coat and shaken the rainwater off her umbrella in the covered area just outside. A few minutes earlier, he had chosen a small, low table alongside the wine bar in the Old Treasury Building's imposing hall, its high ceiling and marbled floor evoking a bygone era. The tables of the wine bar spilled out into the main hall, a multitude of conversations reverberating unintelligibly around him, fuelling his anxiety.

Aresh stood up and she spotted him, her self-confident smile putting him at ease. He gestured awkwardly towards his table and, as she approached, he said, "It's nice to see you. Awful weather, isn't it?"

Cathy sat down. "Cats and dogs. How are you? How's King Eddie's managing without me?"

"It's definitely not the same. I've missed you being around."

She looked directly into his eyes and laughed. "Has no one else noticed?"

Aresh laughed, a little nervously, and changed tack. "How's your study going?"

They settled into a more relaxed conversation and ordered a glass of wine each. Conversation quickly turned to Aresh's efforts to locate his former flatmate.

"I can't remember his first name and I cannot locate any pharmacist whose name I even vaguely recognise on the website of a dozen Sydney hospitals. I don't even know if he's still working as a hospital pharmacist or if I'd recognise his name if he was. Say what you want," Aresh smiled, more than a little nervous, "but I just can't remember anything useful about him."

"And Lisa? What about her?"

"Same story, really. She wasn't a hospital worker, I remember that, but I have no idea how to track her down. I'm confident she'd know who the artist is. You know I feel a bit diffident about it. If I do locate Lisa, I'd be obliged to admit to having taken the painting."

"And return it, if she wants it back."

"Yes. That too."

"Were there any other people in that flat? Anyone who might have remembered at least someone's surname? Come on Aresh. This is about more than whether or not you get to keep that painting."

"I wouldn't have brought the painting into Mark's gallery in the first place if I didn't want to finally figure it all out, okay?" He stopped himself for a moment, conscious he was again sounding defensive. "But, honestly, the only name I really remember is the other flatmate, Allon Cohen. He was a medical student and the flat belonged to his uncle. I tried to contact Allon straight after our visit to the gallery, but I couldn't find him. I even rang his uncle who told me that Allon never finished medical school and shot off to London. He's become an investment banker. I asked the uncle if he had any records of who'd rented the place, even records of me. He just laughed."

"Did he at least give you Allon's contact details in London?"

"Nope. The relationship with that uncle is pretty much finished, I would say. It's a dead end, I promise you."

By the time they had finished their drinks, it was already past the time to head through to the restaurant. Aresh had chosen the Petition Kitchen preferring its less formal atmosphere. Having been guided to their table and presented with their menus, Cathy spoke first. "Aresh, I'm not someone who tends to pull my punches. So, I'm just going to get it out there. You're a good-looking guy, you know, the epitome of eligible. But you've never married, I'm assuming you're currently single. What am I not getting?"

"I could ask the same about you."

"And I'll be happy to tell you, and I'll be as honest as I can. But I asked first."

Aresh exhaled, simultaneously attracted to, yet feeling trapped by Cathy's honesty. "I have had a couple of serious relationships, you know, ones that lasted a long time."

Cathy said nothing.

Unconsciously, Aresh tugged on his shirt collar. "I actually don't really know why I've never settled down with anyone. I've never been the playboy type. Honestly. I suppose it's something to do with coming from an Indian family. I know it's important to my parents that I marry into an Indian family."

"Do you think that's what you'll ultimately do?"

"Marry an Indian girl? Both of my siblings have."

Again, Cathy remained silent.

"OK. If I ever do ask someone to marry me, or if I ever say yes to someone who asks me to marry them, it'll be because I love them not because they're Indian. Or Hindu. Or anything else at all."

They were interrupted by the waiter who explained the specials. They concentrated on the menus for a minute and made their orders. Cathy spoke. "Where are your parents?"

"Dad died a while back, in his late fifties, of ischaemic heart disease. Mum still lives in New Delhi. I go back every December for a few weeks, travel permitting. There's nearly always some family wedding on and it's nice to catch up with everyone."

"Are you waiting for your mum to give you her blessing to marry someone?"

Now Aresh was silent.

Smiling, Cathy demanded. "Tell me—please—that you have at least spoken to her about this stuff."

Aresh blushed, his olive complexion unable to disguise his embarrassment. "I admit it. I'm a coward. It's not a topic I can easily speak about with her. Can I call time out?" He tried to smile and took a gulp of cold water.

"Sorry. That was probably one punch too many. Actually, that's been *my* problem. Getting to the truth of people's feelings—or trying to—has gotten me out of a number of relationships. I can't seem to cope with even the slightest, most innocent self-deception. It's been a deal breaker for me. In the worst sense."

"I can see how that might be the case." Aresh raised his eyebrows. "That's a shame, really. That being honest turns out to be a problem. I mean, my thing about my family has been a huge obstacle for me. I know I'm deceiving myself."

"And your girlfriends."

Cathy's statement, at once accusatory and probing, hung in the air.

"This is definitely not the conversation I expected to be having tonight," said Aresh, forcing a smile. "I feel like the Fellowship candidate, not you. Tell me about your family."

Cathy had been brought up in the Wheatbelt town of Bencubbin, her parents owning and running a wheat and sheep farm that had been in her father's family for decades. She was the middle of three sisters who'd all done well at school having attended a boarding school in Perth. As she started to describe her early years after qualifying from medical school in Perth, their food arrived, the quick service providing them both with much-needed respite.

"Bon Appetit," Aresh said.

"You too." Cathy raised her cutlery preparing to eat, then fixing Aresh in serious regard. "You're a nice guy, Aresh, I really do like you. But, with me, you know, it's the truth, the whole truth and nothing but the truth. We're both grown-ups. I don't want to start anything that's doomed from the beginning, ok?"

Aresh nodded. They ate their tasty meals, giving them both time for thought, and good reason for Aresh to hope for a change of topic. They both passed on dessert. Sipping on her tea, their dinner-date close to a somewhat premature end, Cathy seemed distracted.

"What's on your mind?" asked Aresh. He knew that he had also been a bit subdued.

"At the time you … came by that painting, were you in a relationship?"

Aresh thought for a moment. "I was. Zoe Dickinson was her name. A surgical ward nurse at the Royal Women's. I definitely ran away from that one."

"So, you remember *her* name. Was she one of those serious ones?"

"She was. She was … yes, I remember her for sure."

Cathy nodded, as if processing Aresh's response, then added. "I suspect you know where *she* is then?"

Aresh narrowed his eyes but said nothing.

"I thought so," said Cathy. "I'd bet that she remembers a whole lot more than you do."

Chapter 10
Monday, 29 May 2023

Mark and Pat poured over the images in front of them. Once again, they were in Pat's Welshpool warehouse, their coffee cups long since emptied. They each had an enlargement of the presumed Brodzky, grainy and somehow less convincing on paper than the image had appeared under a magnifying glass in the painting. And Henry Lew's book was open at a painting entitled "Seated Nude".

"Look at the hair colour and the hairline of the female figures," said Mark. "They seem to match, don't you think? Brodzky has painted himself with a mask and the character on the right has one as well. The figure at the back has his mouth and nose covered but the central woman is plain to see. It's as if the artist is making a point – disguising the three male characters but announcing her presence."

Pat blinked, his expression impassive. Mark continued. "According to Lew's book, 1934 is the year Brodzky's marriage finally ended and Bertha, his wife, returned to New York. And it's also the year that an Australian woman called Rachel Blazov turned up in London and sought him out, expecting to meet both Brodzky and his wife. But Bertha was gone and, according to Lew, Rachel and Horace went on to be friends. She even modelled for some of his paintings."

Mark explained how Blazov had bequeathed eight small works by Brodzky to the National Gallery of Victoria after her death in 1979. "I think that unmasked woman in this painting is the same person as the seated nude. And that she is Rachel Blazov."

Pat frowned. "Those two female characters might be the same person, Mark, but that doesn't mean that either of them is Rachel Blazov. I've already shown this image to Richard McNab," looking up at Mark as if to emphasise the authority of his respected colleague's opinion. "He doesn't recognise this painting. He agrees that the character on the right is supposed to be Brodzky, but he couldn't make out the others in any useful detail at all. Maybe the woman is meant to be his wife? Maybe she was some other contact he had in the London art scene? Richard never mentioned anyone called Rachel Blazov." Pat narrowed his eyes and lowered his voice. "Personally, I think the unmasked woman could have been a model Brodzky used from time to time. Maybe it's the same model he painted in the seated nude?"

"Maybe. But he used masks to disguise three of the characters and made no effort to disguise *her*," Mark said, pointing at the red head in the image and glaring at Pat. "Anyway, there are hardly any images of Blazov on the internet and I haven't been able to track down that family name in Australia. I did find a solitary black and white photo of her and Brodzky in thick winter coats, taken outside the Tate in London in 1935, and she did look, well, shorter and rounder than in these paintings. And you can't see her hairline in the photo."

Pat looked dubious, but Mark pressed on. "One of the paintings Blazov gave the NGV is of a group of four figures painted in 1959. By then, he'd have been in his early seventies and she, maybe, sixty. Amongst those four figures is a short, plump woman with sandy, orange hair and a distinctive hairline. And I think that is also Blazov." Mark searched for a reaction, but his mentor's expression remained blank.

"Obviously, she's a lot older than in this painting of masked figures. For what it's worth, Pat, I think that the central figure in this masked ball scene is Rachel Blazov, and Brodzky has used the painting to boldly announce their relationship. I admit I don't know anything about Bertha or any of the models Brodzky used. I've obviously got more research to do."

Pat responded, quiet but firm. "I also sent the image of this painting to Henry Lew in Melbourne, and he got back to me straight away. He agrees that it appears to have been fashioned in the style of a Brodzky. But he's never seen this particular painting so we can't assume it's real. He agrees that the figure on the left is at least meant to be Horace Brodzky. He just didn't know who the other characters might be. It's all too indistinct. He's in touch with Brodzky's son in London who is still alive and still 'with it' in his late nineties. Henry promised to send it to him for his opinion."

Pat caught his breath, slowing down a little as he locked Mark's gaze. "But you need to remember that the main painting we're looking at is of a scene that we don't know for sure is real, meaning that this other little painting might not be a real Brodzky at all. To be honest, it's almost certain that this "Rape on the

Hill" is the work of some unheralded artist who is simply paying his or her respects to Brodzky by including an imagined work by him. Those three other figures—including that unmasked woman—are probably nothing more than figments of the artist's imagination."

Mark was silent, scratching his beard as he digested the warning contained in Pat's words. No doubt, he tended to get overly intense about this sort of thing. For sure, he would take on board whatever Brodzky's son made of the image. But he knew, even if only for his own satisfaction, he had to find out everything he could about Rachel Blazov.

Chapter 11
Tuesday, 30 May 2023

Aresh had never experienced a first date quite as confronting and discouraging. He was attracted to Cathy, but her directness had been disconcerting. Likewise, her expectations of emotional honesty played into his deepest insecurities. Their conversation had exposed him as superficial, even cowardly in his relationships, characteristics he was gradually coming to recognise in himself. And that he did not like.

Worse still, the way she had seen through him had been effortless. He planned to ask her out again, keen to explore the possibility of a more substantial and enduring relationship. For now, he needed to summon resolve for a separate task. He dialled the number and prayed for courage.

"This is Bondi Medical. Our receptionists are currently all busy but please do not hang up as we will get to you as soon as possible." The recorded message continued with the standard warning for suspected emergencies to attend the nearest hospital ED, and a request for those with respiratory symptoms to wear properly fitted surgical masks in the waiting room. The message concluded, "Our receptionists will be with you as soon as possible." Music followed, Amy Winehouse singing something soulful and melodic, Aresh noted. But the sound of Zoe's voice on the message had been unmistakeable and unsettling.

"Thank you for waiting. This is Nikki. How can I help you?"

"Yes, thanks Nikki. My name is Dr Aresh Mehta, I'm a …. a doctor. I'm trying to make contact with Mrs Soltani, Zoe Soltani. Is she in the rooms today?"

Cathy had been on the mark. Aresh had followed Zoe's social media profile ever since they'd broken up—it had bordered on stalking for a few years—and knew that she had ultimately married the Royal Women's heartthrob medico, Amir Soltani. Amir had topped his year at the University of New South Wales. He had toyed with a career in Obstetrics but had followed his second great love,

General Practice, into a successful career running a multi-disciplinary clinic in busy, affluent Bondi where he was now well-established. He'd married his first great love, the irresistible Zoe Dickinson, tall, extremely beautiful and, back in 2010, utterly disillusioned with her previous choice in men, Aresh.

As the seconds ticked by, Aresh's confidence began to waver, no longer sure that he wanted Zoe to be at work after all.

"Just one minute," said Nikki. Aresh looked at his watch. He was fitting this call in between patients in his Tuesday morning clinic and he was getting anxious that he was falling even further behind. His clinics were always busy, more because of the time he spent with each patient than the large numbers of them. Their circumstances were often complex and the cancers so many of them had demanded calm and patient explanation.

"Aresh, now this is a surprise."

Aresh smiled, an automatic response. "Hello Zoe. Thank you so much for taking this call. I imagine your rooms are frantic."

"And I suppose you're just sitting on your hands over there in Perth, Mr Maharajah?"

He smiled even more broadly, their knowledge of each other's past as well as their current whereabouts testament to a lasting if neglected connection. "Yes, I'm pretty busy too. I'll get straight to the point, but it is just so nice to hear your voice, Zo. I have no excuses, you know. I was an idiot. And how's your Persian Prince?"

Zoe laughed. To many of her friends, her choice in men had represented a sort of Asian theme, but the two colleagues could hardly have been more different.

"He's doing just fine. Now, how can I help?"

Aresh recounted the story of the painting that had been intended for Lisa. He'd kept possession of it all these years but was now trying to track her down to see if she knew who had painted it and if she wanted it for herself.

"I remember that awful painting. It was positively scary. Not giving that back to Lisa doesn't sound like too bad a wrong to be trying to right, after all this time. Are you OK?"

"No, no. I'm fine. Truly. But I've become interested in art. And I suppose I'm trying to prove something to myself by identifying the artist who painted it and then, you know, returning it to Lisa."

"Sounds to me like you might be trying to prove something to somebody else as well."

Aresh sighed at his evident transparency. "Yes, that too. You wouldn't remember Lisa's surname by any chance?"

"Lisa Dimopoulos. She was Juan's girlfriend. You remember him. He was a pharmacist. And she was doing a media studies degree. She let him go him just before we broke up. I think she realised that he wasn't her type. She's done some journalism. Done some writing. But I haven't actually seen her since that time."

"How'd you know all that?"

"How'd you know where to find me?"

"Sure, but I had good reason to … follow you."

"And I like to follow lots of people, Aresh. Lisa was always interesting. Didn't you think?"

"Zo, the more I think about things, the more I realise how ensconced in my own self-centred bubble I've been my whole life. I couldn't remember Juan's first name let alone Lisa's surname. I did remember Allon," he added in mock triumph. "Apparently, he's in London. But I couldn't pinpoint him either."

"He's hyphenated his surname if you really want to contact him."

Aresh laughed. "No thanks, I think Lisa's the person I need to speak to. Can you spell her surname for me, and I'll leave you alone?"

"Please don't do that, Aresh. I'd love to stay in touch. I'll send you an email – you've got a 'health' email address I presume?"

"Thanks Zoe. Yes. It's 'Aresh-dot-Mehta at health'. And I'll write back and tell you what I've been up to." As if she doesn't already know, he thought. "You do the same, please. Tell me about Amir and what you've all been doing."

Within an hour of ending the call, Zoe had sent him Lisa's name and a link to her latest journalistic endeavour: a podcast entitled 'The Female Voice'.

Chapter 12
Tuesday, 25 October 1960

Since her first "sojourn in Chelsea"—as Horace's inscription on one of the artworks he had gifted her back in 1937 had described their affair—Rachel had returned to Europe for extended periods on several occasions. This time, however, with Horace well into his seventies, more discontent than ever at his lack of recognition within the art world, and with his current accommodation in Kilburn somehow colder and dingier than she'd encountered on previous visits, she felt the last threads of her devotion to him dissolving.

Moreover, her sister Bernice had just been diagnosed with pancreatic cancer and, according to her nephew Sam's distressed telegram message, she'd been given only months to live. The two sisters had always been close despite the different politics—and paths in life—they had pursued. Bernice was three years older than Rachel and had married her childhood sweetheart, Paul Greenbatt, at twenty-one. She had studied accountancy but, initially unable to fall pregnant, had buried herself in the Blazov real estate business, becoming integral to its operations, her father David's obvious and uncontested successor.

By contrast, from her early teens, Rachel had acquired a strong social conscience. She had complied with her parents' wishes to study one of the health professions, becoming a physiotherapist. To their dismay, however, at about the same age her older sister had married, Rachel joined the local branch of the Communist party. On this overcast October morning, as Rachel descended the steps onto the tarmac at Melbourne airport, she reflected upon her earliest contact with Horace's brother Bob at one of her first party meetings. His eloquence had been thrilling and had helped reinforce her confidence in the veracity of her evolving political beliefs. It had been precisely that eloquence and wit that she had found so attractive in Horace.

Against all expectations, Bernice and Paul had conceived, and Sam was born in 1936 while Rachel was happily ensconced in Chelsea. Sam's unforeseen arrival was greeted with predictable joy by the respective families, the sisters' ageing parents in particular. Uneasy about the rising political instability in Europe and haunted by David's painful memories of his youth in Poland, Rachel decided to leave London, come home and see her family and her treasured nephew.

But the joy of Sam's arrival proved short-lived. Paul became unwell in early 1939, his son just two years old, and rapidly succumbed to what was thought to be a brain tumour. David was tragically killed in a tram accident while walking his dog on William Street in 1943. And their mother, Ruth, fell ill with influenza and died in May 1946. By that time, Rachel was working in Germany as assistant to the Chief Welfare Officer of the British Occupation Zone, having jumped at her first opportunity to return to Europe. In the space of a little over six years, the family had been halved, Rachel had gone back to Europe and Bernice had been left very much alone, as sole parent and head of the family's expanding business interests.

Rachel returned briefly to Melbourne in 1948 to touch base with her family, before being enticed once again to Europe and to Horace in London. But, like Horace, their relationship had also lost some of its spark. Caught between her loyalties to her sister and nephew in Melbourne, and to noisy, chaotic, multi-cultural London to which she was, like her late father, so drawn, she had travelled back and forth between the two, always unsettled, never completely at home.

Now, Bernice was dying, Sam was barely twenty and Rachel's presence to support him was needed. She understood that, at almost sixty years of age, she would not likely ever be returning to London or Horace. Sensing the finality of this farewell, Horace had gifted her one last painting, a group of four human figures in which she had been included. The truthful manner in which Horace had depicted her appearance in this painting offered stark evidence of the depredations of the twenty-five years since they had first met. It was a fine contrast to the painting, also including four human figures, he'd given her over twenty years earlier and which she had, in turn, gifted to Sam.

She entered the airport terminal, this latest present from Horace tucked under her arm for safe keeping. She looked around and, in an instant, spotted her nephew who had come to collect her.

Chapter 13
Wednesday, 21 July 2010

Sam Green loved his study. In it, he felt secure, enveloped by its dark, wood-panelled walls and shelves, covered by certificates and awards and packed with books and ornaments accumulated over decades of achievement and success in business. His desk was wide and deep yet always uncluttered, his essential documents organised efficiently inside the built-in filing cabinets behind it. His chair, understated in size, was made of the softest Italian leather, pointing to his preference for quality over quantity in all things.

Around the walls he had assembled some of his favourite paintings even if not his most valuable. They resonated with him in a way that few observers, only the most learned students of Australian fine art, might appreciate. This was his refuge, where he felt most at home.

It grieved him to sully this sanctuary with the presence of Raymond Chalmers and with the subject of their meeting. Sam would have drawn the line with his son, firm and clear, but Elizabeth had managed to persuade him otherwise, as she always did. Bradley had become a recurring source of stress for the family, his natural charm and good looks matched only by his laziness and sense of entitlement. That Brad had mistreated many of the young women in his life including his own wife was a source of dismay and disappointment to Sam; that his son had now extended this mistreatment to the point of risking imprisonment was shameful and, to his mind, should have commanded suitable punishment.

He forced himself to concentrate upon what Raymond Chalmers was saying.

"This can all be sorted, Mr Green. But that will require an immediate decision on your part."

"What do I have to do?"

"Just give me the word and I will take care of everything."

"I'm not sure I know how these things work, Mr Assistant Commissioner."

"And let's keep it that way. May I call you Sam?"

A cold chill travelled through Sam Green's body, the thought of being obliged to relate to this man on a first-name basis was galling, Sam's thin smile as close to saying 'yes' as he could manage. "I am asking what *you* will need from me."

"It will require some cash and perhaps some assets, but nothing you cannot afford. I haven't dealt with many of your kind before, but I know that you all stick together and I'm sure there are plenty of them you can lean on for assistance if you need it."

Sam chose not to take the bait. He had been warned that the Assistant Commissioner, approaching retirement, was vile to his core and unashamedly driven by greed, eager to bolster his already considerable affluence. "It will still be necessary to agree upon the details Mr Chalmers," the use of his surname intended as a rebuke.

"No need to be short with me, my friend. I wouldn't be here if you didn't need me." Chalmers smiled. "It will be one million dollars—in cash and in this study—and," he made a show of looking around the room, admiring the sumptuous décor at his leisure, "perhaps a small gift as well. I suspect you won't even notice the difference. If you agree, I shall start immediately." He extended his hand for Sam to shake.

Defeated, Sam Green reciprocated.

Chapter 14
Tuesday, 30 May 2023

Mark opened the gallery and settled at his computer to interrogate some of the numerous websites that provided access to historical documents now well-and-truly in the public domain. Despite Pat's admonition, he remained committed to his theory that the unmasked woman in what he was referring to as "the Brodzky painting" was the same Rachel Blazov mentioned in Henry Lew's book. Amongst the drawings and paintings that were included in her bequest to the National Gallery of Victoria in 1979, one of the works dating from 1935 to 1937 bore an inscription by Brodzky in dedication to Rachel Blazov, and another was a delicate line drawing of a female nude. His partner, Linda, had made a direct interpretation.

"It is inconceivable that any artist, even in this day and age let alone a hundred years ago, would gift a female nude to any woman who was not the subject of that drawing. That drawing will be of Rachel Blazov," she'd said. And if that was true—and Linda was rarely wrong about these things—Mark also knew that it was plausible that the painting entitled "Seated Nude" from 1951 that appeared in Lew's book could also be of Rachel Blazov. To Mark's eye, there was a distinct resemblance between the central female figures of the two works. It was just that he didn't know if that specific female figure resembled Rachel Blazov. Unfortunately, the detail of the nude in the line drawing didn't help at all.

There was a lot of material online for Mark to sift through, much of it repetitious, and he was soon engrossed in the strange rhythm of online searching, regularly wandering off on unrelated tangents. A phone call caught him by surprise, causing him to scramble to answer it. It was from former medical colleague and well-known art collector, Phillip Allbrook, who had a query about an additional tax he'd had to pay on a painting he'd just sold at auction. Mark never ceased to be amazed how at ease people could feel calling him with a question about a work of art they'd bought or sold—or were planning to buy or sell—from someone other than him.

Mark explained the basic idea behind the resale royalty tax – that the person selling a painting today had to forego a percentage of the sale price to the original artist, and that this applied each time that work of art was sold, even if the painting had decreased in value. They agreed that this made no more sense than a current homeowner foregoing a percentage of the proceeds of the sale of their house to the original owner every time that house changed hands.

He brought the conversation to as gentle a conclusion as he possibly could. "That is the world we live in, Phil. Trading in art can work, but it takes lots of patience to allow any work of art to appreciate. You need plenty of luck to pick the artists and the specific works that will do that. And the resale royalty hasn't helped the seller one bit."

The disgruntled collector ended the call with rueful thanks allowing Mark to return to his research. There was plenty of information in old Melbourne newspapers about the Blazov real estate business although little detail about the family. One newspaper clipping noted the death of founder David Blazov in a tram accident in 1943; another the death of Ruth Blazov, presumably his wife, in 1946. There was a marriage notice for a Bernice Blazov, daughter of David and Ruth, to Paul Greenbatt in 1921, published in a weekly production called the Hebrew Standard of Australasia.

Rachel appeared in a number of newspaper segments. She was born in 1903. Some school age achievements were documented, quaint reminders of a radically different era. And another about a dress she wore, possibly to a debutante ball. She was variably described as a physiotherapist, a welfare worker and a refugee worker; and a spinster. Her bequest to the NGV following her death in 1979 was highlighted in several entries.

Her travel to Germany in 1945, at the end of the second world war, attracted commentary when she and the other welfare workers were given what must have been exceptional visa exemptions to allow them to enter Europe so soon after the end of the war. She returned from Germany in 1948 and spoke to a number of community groups in Melbourne before leaving again shortly afterwards. Later still, she appeared on the Australian electoral roll living in Eltham, north-east of Melbourne in 1954 and again from 1961 onwards.

He could find no obituary for her but the impression of an independent woman, committed to the greater good and with a restless passion for Europe emerged loud and clear for Mark.

Disappointingly, a search of Horace Brodzky online found less material than was contained in Lew's biography. Save for a description of six aerogrammes written to Rachel Blazov by Horace Brodzky between 1961 and 1968 held by the State Library of Victoria, proving beyond doubt the ongoing close contact between the artist and, Mark imagined, his muse. The photograph with Horace outside the Tate had been taken in 1935; the aerogrammes from the nineteen sixties proved that Rachel and Horace had remained dear to each other for more than three decades, right up until Brodzky's death in 1969. The aerogrammes were said to include ink drawings produced for Rachel's benefit. Mark made a note to track them down when he next visited his other daughter, Rebecca, and her family in Melbourne.

He searched Alfred Brodney, known as Bob, who had been born in Melbourne, had left Australia with the family before he had turned ten, and had returned to Australia and studied law. He'd been a significant figure in the fledgling Communist party in Melbourne and later became a much-respected industrial relations lawyer. He had married but had no children. Seven years older than Rachel, Mark could only imagine that the two had met in the context of their shared political leanings.

Based upon what he now knew about Horace and Rachel, he could construct a credible timeline that described a connection, much of it purposeful, often intimate, between the two Melburnians, spanning thirty-five years. Yet there was a vacuum of information from Rachel's death to the present.

At that moment, the gallery door opened, and an elderly couple entered and took some tentative steps towards his desk. Mark closed his laptop – his investigation of the Blazov family would have to wait.

Chapter 15
Wednesday, 31 May 2023

The podcast episode Aresh listened to was excellent. It was one of a series of interviews with emerging authors across a variety of genres but all of them women under thirty years of age. Lisa would be in her mid-thirties by now, he guessed. The emphasis was current and topical, skewed towards issues of gender identity and sexual orientation more so than strident feminism. But all seemed like fascinating authors from diverse backgrounds, many of whom had lived the experiences about which they had chosen to write.

He thought he recognised Lisa's voice. In the photos of her available online she seemed thinner and more angular than he had remembered, her hairstyle and tattoos pointing to what Zoe had inferred when she'd described Lisa as "interesting". He had had no inclination back in 2010. And it was clearer to him than ever that he had not been on Zoe's wavelength. Back then, it really had been all about him.

Dear Lisa

Thanks for your terrific podcast. I've just binged your young authors series and it was engaging and informative. I loved it.

You might not recall me but we did, very briefly, share an apartment in Coogee back in 2010 when you and Juan were an item. I tracked down Zoe Dickinson (my ex from that time) and she pointed me in your direction. I've gone on to complete Obstetrics and Gynaecology and I'm now in Perth as a specialist in Gynae Oncology (surgery).

I'm not sure how to broach this without condemning myself, but here goes. When you left Sydney for good that weekend, someone left a painting outside our apartment which was meant for you. Whoever you sent to clean out your apartment a little while later left it behind. I don't know if they didn't realise if they were meant to take it or if they looked at it and decided it wasn't fit to be taken. It's a pretty confronting image. Whichever way, it wasn't claimed, I couldn't contact you (and I really did try – for a while) and I have sort of taken it with me across the country ever since.

I don't know who it's by and I'm finally trying to find out. And then have the painting returned to you or the artist, assuming either of you want it back.

I apologise for this bolt from the blue but wonder if you'd be prepared to look at the painting and help me find the artist. I'm reasonably sure that it's not valuable but you never know.

Best wishes (and thanks again for the great podcast),

Aresh Mehta

Aresh
My recollection is as hazy as yours. But thanks for your positive feedback. I think I had better see the image. Can you send it to me?

Aresh sent the image and within minutes Lisa replied.
Thanks for sending it through. Can we speak soon?

Lisa's mobile number was beneath her other business contact details at the foot of her emails. Aresh rang as soon as he got into his car to drive home from work.

"Lisa Dimopoulos speaking."

"Hi. Lisa. It's Aresh Mehta in Perth. Nice to speak after all these years."

"Yes, me too. Look, I'm a bit unnerved by that painting. The artist was a friend of mine at that time. Her name was Angie Richards."

The name meant nothing to Aresh. "How do you know that Angie was the artist? It's not signed anywhere."

"Because she's painted herself as the victim."

"Jesus. Sorry. We wondered if that might be the case, the artist outing the rapist, as it were. Do you know if this really happened? And did she pursue the guy?"

Lisa exhaled. "Angie died the same weekend I left Coogee. There was a fire in her home studio." Another deep breath. "She must have dropped the painting off maybe a matter of an hour or two after I left. She was actually doing quite well. Paintings from that same series of works were just being exhibited at a nice gallery in Woollahra. She was getting regular commissions, mainly for portraits. She was talented."

Aresh was trying to get the pieces of this story to fit together. He turned left close to the site of the old football stadium, now a building site for a residential development, driving over the railway bridge and preparing to turn right onto Railway Parade. "Do you recognise the man in the mask?"

"No. No idea. I don't recognise anything except her, although she's included lots of other details, as if she's giving us clues to his identity. But then why the mask? I definitely didn't see this painting at the opening of her exhibition. I'd have remembered it for sure. She must have kept it back. It was a pretty dark exhibition – paintings about murder, suicide, all pretty violent as I recall. Nothing I would ever hang at home."

"We think the mask might be a reference to the little painting she's included over on the far-left wall. All four characters are wearing or holding masks too."

"Sorry, I can't see that much detail in this image. Do you really think that's significant? And who else is looking at this when you say 'we'?"

"I showed this painting to a couple of art experts here in Perth about a fortnight ago and they're working—well, we're all working—on the hypothesis that the events depicted in the painting are real. We wanted to figure out who the artist was and who the people in it are. And what happened to them. But I suppose most of that is solved now. The victim was Angie Richards. And she died a matter of months after she made this painting."

"I'm feeling very uneasy about this, Aresh. Why did Angie leave this painting out of the exhibition? It certainly fits with the theme of that exhibition. And why didn't she just keep it herself? Why did she give it to me? Was she afraid that someone else was going to see it? You know what I'm thinking. You must be wondering the same thing."

Aresh was waiting patiently to cross Cambridge Street, looking left and right for a break in the traffic. "I need to piece all this together. It is a bit worrying. We're still trying to locate that little painting on the study wall. We hope it'll point us to the man in the mask." He eased out onto Cambridge and then sped across when the traffic cleared. "I don't suppose you remember the name of the gallery where Angie held that exhibition?"

"Galerie Strauss, as I recall. In Woollahra. I don't know if it's still open. I've got a small team of investigators who work on my podcasts. They might be able to track down some more details. I'll get them onto it, and I'll let you know if we get any answers."

"Thanks Lisa. And I'll call you too as soon as we dig up anything new." He had come to a stop in his carport as the call with Lisa ended. He turned off the engine and sat quietly for a couple of minutes, processing the conversation. Alongside the driveway, a row of hydrangeas stood verdant but flowerless, the colourful promise of summer still months away.

That the rape depicted in Angie Richard's painting might have been a real event had always seemed, to Aresh, a distinct possibility. But was this murder as well?

Chapter 16
Thursday, 1 June 2023

Drenching rain was falling just as Pat and Mark eased into their regular South Perth café booth, lucky to have escaped the onset of the downpour. Olivia was working in Beaufort Street while Pat now had a full complement of staff in his warehouse, the workforce crisis of the preceding years having begun to ease.

"How'd the sale end up?" asked Mark.

Pat and Helen's annual autumn sale earlier that week had been a strong one but, as usual, a number of works had been passed in and remained available for purchase for a short while longer. "We did well. That early Arthur Boyd sold the day after the sale. And to the same person who'd made such a fuss about it during the preview, but who refused to make a bid on the night. I was looking straight at him, and he just blinked at me." Pat smiled, bemused, as always, by the unpredictable behaviour of art buyers. "In the end, we only had to take half a dozen pieces back to Welshpool."

Mark changed tack as their coffees arrived. "I've found out quite a bit about the woman I think is in that Brodzky painting." He couldn't interpret Pat's silence but took it as an invitation to expand upon his theory. That Brodzky and Blazov had an intimate relationship was, as far as Mark was concerned, incontestable. And the works she bequeathed to the NGV as well as the aerogrammes described on the family tree website pointed to the enduring nature of that relationship. Rachel Blazov had had no children, but she did have a sister, Bernice, who had married into the Greenbatt family and had taken over her family business at around the time her husband had died.

"Bernice had just one child, a son named Sam. It isn't clear exactly when, but sometime in the nineteen sixties the Blazov real estate company was sold, and Green Enterprises appeared. They were property developers and they expanded into the lucrative Sydney market. There's a death notice for Bernice from January 1961 so I'm assuming that Sam took over the whole thing in his early twenties. He moved the entire business base to Sydney, I think, around nineteen seventy or seventy-one. There's been little about Sam Green in the press for the last five or so years but there's been no death notice, so I think he's still alive at about eighty-six or seven."

"How did you get all that?"

Mark explained the various historical and family tree websites that contained copies of a huge range of documents and publications. It was laborious and there was plenty of duplication but there was a lot that could be unearthed. "We know that Rachel Blazov bequeathed eight works by Horace Brodzky to the NGV all of which can be seen online and none of which is our Brodzky painting. But Rachel might have had other paintings by him. No one we know who is familiar with Brodzky seems to recognise this particular work. Maybe it is a real work that was given to her sister and then to her nephew. Maybe it really was hanging in his study."

Pat blew over the steaming coffee cup and put it down. "The masked man with the surgical scar can't be Sam Green. That scene was painted in around 2010, wasn't it, at which time Green would have been over seventy. It's definitely not him."

"I agree. But Green has a son, Bradley, and a daughter, Sarah. Maybe our masked man is Bradley or even Sarah's partner, if she had one back then? Look, Pat, I appreciate that this is just a theory based on an idea based on a whim. But the connection between Brodzky, the Blazovs and the Greens might mean something. And whoever painted the rape scene is an artist who had the technical skill not only to portray a crime, real or imaginary, and with great power, but who could easily have also had the artistic composure to appreciate a small masterpiece of international art hanging on the study wall and understand how it might identify the scene."

Pat sat very still for what seemed to Mark like a long time, before he spoke. "OK. Let's assume you're right. What's your next move?"

They chatted for another half an hour, Mark outlining his plan to keep milling the websites for information about the various characters contributing to this evolving scenario, before they left the café and headed back to their respective offices. The sky remained overcast, but the rain had stopped, and the threat of another deluge seemed to have passed.

As Mark drove onto the freeway overpass at Como, his thoughts were dominated by his theories about the painting—about both paintings—and he felt himself being drawn back in time, to Brodzky and to pre-war London. As the ramp rose upwards and curved to the right, the clouds and river in front of him seemed to merge, forming a striking and ominous backdrop, and creating the sensation that he was about to take flight over the Swan River. The ringing of his telephone brought him back to full concentration as he followed the tight bend of the descent and negotiated his way across the Mitchell Freeway towards the far-right lane.

"Hi Mark, It's Aresh Mehta."

"Good morning Aresh. How are you? I think we're making some progress on that Brodzky painting. Have you found anything?"

"I'm good thanks Mark. I've located that old roommate, Lisa, and she has identified the artist of the painting as her friend Angie Richards, who she says has painted herself as the victim. She was a bit of a rising star in the Sydney art scene, Lisa said, and this particular painting was almost certainly one of a series of similarly confronting works that were being exhibited in a Woollahra gallery right at the same time the painting was left outside our apartment."

Aresh paused to catch his breath just as Mark approached the Charles Street exit. "So, this is a self-portrait of her being raped?" Mark asked.

"Yes, that seems to be the case. Although we don't know if the event actually took place. But Lisa told me that Angie died in an accidental studio fire on the same weekend she left the painting with us in Coogee, the same weekend that Lisa walked out of the apartment for good. We both wondered … I mean, it occurred to both of us, that the fire might not have been an accident."

The traffic light arrow turned green, and Mark turned onto Vincent Street. "Surely that fire will have been thoroughly investigated, Aresh? Although I suppose it would do no harm to check. I have to admit that I've never heard of Angie Richards, but I'll see what I can find out about her. I wonder if we might need to raise this with the Sydney police. It seems to be a bit bigger than just the search for the origins of a painting."

"Yes, you may be right. As it turns out, Lisa is a podcaster and has some people who work for her who can do some of that digging. I'm hoping she'll have something for us later this week. Shall we get together this weekend? In your gallery again?"

*****

Greta McCartney's morning had been effective but uninspiring, interviewing a medical secretary who, after little probing, admitted to stealing cash from her employer, a popular but gullible cardiologist. The office accounting system had captured every fraudulent act, convincing the doctor that there had been a crime and prompting him to contact the Fraud Squad. The secretary had resigned on the spot, but the bewildered specialist still had to decide whether or not to press charges. Greta had left her contact details should he need further assistance.

Greta's move to the Fraud Squad had been a body blow after what she had thought had been a promising career in the Major Crime Squad. After three years in her current role and approaching forty years of age, she had been forced to accept that she would not likely progress much further. Although her demotion had been explained to her as being for reasons of her own welfare, she had little doubt that she had been punished for being outspoken, possibly a little too principled and undoubtedly far too naïve. More and more, she wondered if her long term future lay outside the police force.

It was almost time for her second coffee of the morning when her mobile phone rang. "Greta speaking."

"Hi, Greta, it's Lisa Dimopoulos. How're you doing?"

Even though they'd met just once, almost six months earlier, Greta remembered Lisa well. They'd caught up one Sunday afternoon at The Beresford. Lisa, she recalled, was a striking looking woman who had her own podcast every new episode of which Greta had since followed without fail. "I'm well thanks. How are you?"

"Very well. I hope you don't mind me calling like this. You might remember that I have a podcast. And I definitely remember that you're in the police. I wonder if I could arrange a time to meet up again to discuss a … situation that I'm looking into?"

"Of course, I'd love to catch up. I've been following your podcast and it's great. But I might not be able to help you much in terms of any investigation. I'm not really in the thick of things anymore, in the police that is. Still, I might at least be able to point you in the right direction."

"Excellent, I really appreciate it. I don't suppose you are free this week?"

"I haven't … well … my diary is free."

"How about tonight?"

*****

It wasn't even a date, but Greta was fidgety and excited as she waited at the bar for Lisa to appear. She had arrived early and had walked past the building a couple of times, instinctively checking out the area, then scanning the interior space after she'd sat down, always on the look-out for anything out of balance. The time away from serious criminal investigation hadn't blunted her wariness. She just hoped that she could relax enough to enjoy the meeting with Lisa, and not have to disappoint her too much if it became apparent that she wouldn't be able to help. The true crime podcast fashion, if that was what this was about, was not one anyone in the police regarded favourably.

Spot on seven thirty, Lisa walked in, elegant and assured much as Greta had remembered. She spotted Greta and joined her at the bar.

"Thanks for meeting me here" said Lisa as she smiled and extended her hand. Greta stood and they shook hands, Greta appreciating the firmness of Lisa's grip. They moved to a booth and sat down. A waiter took their drink orders and they sat, silent for a moment and held each other's gaze.

"How can I help you?"

"There's a particular event—a fatal house fire from back in 2010—that I'd like to know more about, but I'll tell you the whole story and you can tell me what you think of it." Lisa opened a manila folder removing the image of Angie's painting. "I knew the woman who painted this. She was a friend of mine and she depicted herself as the victim. And she died in that house fire not long afterwards." Lisa continued, describing events from the time of the Coogee apartment through to the call from Aresh Mehta.

Greta listened, intrigued by the story and captivated by the storyteller. She would be able to look for something that might link Angie with a sexual assault at around that time and she could make inquiries into the fire. Chances were that there would be little to be found and even less chance of cooperation from her colleagues, but Lisa's account of events stirred a flicker of concern in the former Major Crime detective. Greta was cautiously curious and not prepared to dismiss the possibility of there being substance to Lisa's concerns. "I'll ask around and let you know. Would you like something to eat? The burgers here are terrific."

"Sure. I'm starving. Let's eat."

Chapter 17
Friday, 2 June 2023

"Dad, I wonder if we can drag you away from that screen?" Olivia was in need of some input into a new inquiry about a little painting that had just been brought in. And she was more than a little concerned that her father was becoming obsessed with his search for the origins of the Sydney painting and that supposed little Brodzky.

"Yes, of course. I've found out some stuff about that studio fire," he said, before appreciating the annoyance in Olivia's expression. "Sorry. I'm 'on the job'," directing his comment at the new client and smiling awkwardly.

"This is Lorne Etherington, dad. Lorne, Mark Lewis. And this," Olivia pointed to a small painting on the easel in front of them "is a work that Lorne has had for about ten years."

The painting appeared to be a work on paper, an abstract series of geometric colour blocks in grey-brown and green with a band of blue, inspiration possibly drawn from De Stael and pointing to the mid-twentieth century era of Australian abstract art. It was signed in neat upper-case letters: "D. O'CONNOR".

"Where did you get this from? It's rather lovely."

"I bought it in a small gallery in Sydney about twenty years ago. My family and I moved to Perth around that time, and it came with us." Lorne was now a senior project manager with a large oil and gas conglomerate. These days, his time was largely his own and he had long wanted to know more about the painting and the artist.

"Have you googled the artist?" Mark asked.

"I did find a Derek O'Connor who is an Australian artist, but nothing on his website resembles this and I just didn't have the gumption to contact him. That was about all I could find."

"OK. Let me do that search for you and see what I come up with. I don't think it's going to be especially valuable, but it would be nice to reconnect it with its maker. You never know. I'll call you as soon as I've sorted it out. Assuming that I can. Either way, it's a nice little picture." Mark smiled. "It could do with a new frame, by the way."

Olivia and the new client exchanged contact details before he departed.

"What have you found out about that fire?" Olivia asked.

"Angie Richards died in a house fire in a Surry Hills apartment on Sunday, 18 July 2010. According to the only newspaper report I could find, published on the following Tuesday, the police were investigating the cause although there were no obviously suspicious circumstances. Neighbours were said to have been unable to help because of the speed and intensity of the fire. Reference was made to her being an artist and to the exhibition at Galerie Strauss in Woollahra, and there is a comment from the gallery principal, Judith Strauss – shocked and distressed as expected."

"Do you know her?"

"Nope. I remember the gallery from magazine advertisements but nothing more."

"Was there any follow-up about the fire? In the news?"

"Not a word. Presumably nothing suspicious was ever found. I found nothing helpful about the exhibition or any of the other works. I hope that the podcaster has some luck there."

"Lisa. Dad, her name's Lisa Dimopoulos. You might like to listen to her. She's very good."

Admonished, Mark headed back to the computer and googled Derek O'Connor.

*****

The gravity of the scene depicted in the painting weighed on Cathy no less than it did on Aresh and the others. She had covered a lot of scientific territory during the preceding week of intense exam study but was feeling burnt out and, despite having decided to keep things with Aresh on hold, she had felt drawn into the search for the truth behind his painting. She searched for Bradley Green and soon appreciated the need for a more refined approach.

Even after limiting her search to newspaper articles and by country and date, the number of citations was large. A number of different Bradley Greens appeared more often than others, and Cathy was soon able to recognise those who were not the person she was looking for and gloss over them.

The Brad Green for whom she was looking seemed to appear only in photographs, in the social columns, very much the young Sydney socialite. He was tall and had a shock of dark, curly hair, not inconsistent with the appearance of the masked rapist Angie Richard's painting. She printed off the image that most resembled the man in the painting, taken at a real estate association event in August 2007 amongst a small group of partygoers. Concentrating on birth notices, she then confirmed that Bradley David Green had been born on 11 May 1978 to Elizabeth and Sam Green at the Prince of Wales Hospital in Randwick; brother to Sarah; proud grandparents were listed as Thomas and Grace Wright.

There was a marriage notice, to Lorraine Smart in 1997, and the birth of two children in 2000 and 2002, Thomas and William. Their divorce was documented too, in 2011. For Cathy, the basic facts of Brad Green's life were forming into a picture that was still indistinct, as if being seen through a misted pane of glass that needed to be wiped clear. She set aside her investigation around six. Several more hours of study awaited her after dinner.

Chapter 18
Sunday, 4 June 2023

After breakfast at Boo Too on Bulwer Street, Linda and Mark drove to the gallery. Helen and Pat joined them there, Pat's recurring back problems warning him off sitting in a coffee shop for any length of time. By nine thirty, Aresh had also arrived; Olivia, her husband Hendrick and their children were heading off to Serpentine for a picnic with some friends.

The group settled around the computer screen as Linda connected them by Zoom to Lisa Dimopoulos in Sydney. Aresh took the lead, introducing Lisa and excusing Cathy on the grounds that she was in the thick of exam study. Then Mark took over, summarising the facts as he knew them and suggesting that they share any new developments. He invited Lisa to go next.

"For starters, I have a contact inside the New South Wales police force, and they found no report of a sexual assault or other incident around that time that might be linked to the painting. If the painting documents a real event, I don't think it was ever reported to police."

Mark wasn't surprised by that but couldn't help wondering how journalists managed to establish these police contacts in the first place. "What about the fire?" he asked.

"Yes, that was a real event. It occurred late on a Sunday night, around nine pm, on Reservoir Street in Surry Hills. It's an old area, Victorian era, terraced houses. Angie Richards was renting a two-storey apartment and the downstairs studio along with most of the upper floor were almost totally destroyed by the blaze. Her body, poor thing, was incinerated and it took dental records to identify her. The Arson Squad concluded that it was an accident, possibly related to a cigarette or similar. The intensity of the fire was attributed to the accelerant effect of turpentine and other painting products."

A sombre shroud of silence settled over the meeting as they all absorbed Lisa's account.

"I assume there were no paintings or drawings found?" Pat asked.

"The impact upstairs was less but it was still extensively damaged. There was no reference to any works of art in the police report."

"I bet she had some art on the walls upstairs. Was that in the report?"

"I'll check again, but the ferocity of the fire was considerable, and I don't think anything flammable would have survived that inferno."

"It still feels like an uncomfortable coincidence to me," said Aresh. "I mean, was she even a smoker? Did she do drugs? I suppose it wouldn't be a huge surprise if she did, but do we know for sure?"

"I never saw her smoke … anything," said Lisa. "The report reached its conclusion in part because of the remnants of a metal cigarette lighter found in the ashes."

"It might not have been hers" Aresh shot back. "You know, there's an old-fashioned cigarette lighter on the study table in Angie's painting. It looks as if it's made of metal." The gallery crew all swivelled to look at the painting, standing on an easel next to them. "I bet that lighter belonged to the household in the painting, or maybe the rapist, rather than the victim. I'm not saying it's the same lighter they found in the fire, but maybe Angie included the lighter in the painting as another clue to the identity of her rapist."

Lisa followed Aresh's train of thought. "So, if the lighter in the painting isn't Angie's, the lighter they found in her burnt-out apartment might not have been hers either."

"He's your killer" hissed Helen, pointing at the masked assailant in the painting. "You might never prove it, but that bloody cigarette lighter was his and he used it as the murder weapon."

They all flinched, as much, on account of Helen's vehemence, Mark thought, as in response to her bold accusation.

Mark addressed his next comments directly to Lisa. "I have an admittedly tenuous theory that the two paintings in the spotlight—Angie's painting and the little Brodzky painting pictured on the study wall—are both connected somehow to the Green family. Are you familiar with Sam Green or Green Enterprises? They're property people whose head office is in Sydney, in the central business district."

"No, but I can find out. Can you tell me anything more about them?"

"Cathy sent me what she's found out about them," said Aresh, Mark sensing that he looked and sounded a little sheepish. "There's a son, Brad Green, who appears regularly in the social columns. For what it's worth, he's tall and has a mop of dark hair."

Lisa nodded her acknowledgement. "Thanks. Can you email me what you've got? I think there's still a whole lot more we need to get clear. I'm trying to track down the DI—the Detective Inspector—who conducted the arson investigation to see if he can recall anything out of the ordinary about the investigation. He retired a few years ago so it might take us a bit longer to locate him. But I'll keep you posted. Mark – we should get together again soon to compare notes."

Mark thanked Lisa and ended the call. The gallery was due to open shortly so tasks for the group for the coming days were assigned before Mark summarised the current status. "I think I need to keep some sense of perspective here. This is only a painting—literally just oil and canvas—the product of a talented artist, no doubt. But it isn't a photograph let alone an official document. And the Green Family are probably all decent folk."

"And wealthy enough to punish anyone who defames them," added Pat under his breath.

"Yes. Of course. So, as much as we all want to figure out what happened here…"

"And convict the culprit," Helen interjected.

"That too," Mark continued, distracted for an instant by Helen's passion and focus. "We just need to tread a little carefully. OK?"

*****

"So that's your Crime Investigation Squad is it?" asked Linda.

It was just the two of them in the gallery now and Mark looked at Linda, in that moment struggling to respond.

"I shouldn't laugh. There's probably something to it all."

"Yes, I suppose it is a little fanciful. But Lisa seems to agree with us. And she's no amateur."

Linda smiled. "I'm not so sure she's a professional in criminality, either. Looks like things didn't work out for Aresh and Cathy."

"How do you know that?"

"How do you *not* know? Honestly, Mark, you couldn't miss it. She'd have been here if they were an item." She paused and caught his eye as if double-checking he wasn't pulling her leg. "I thought they were well suited. It's a shame don't you think?"

"She's studying for her final Fellowship exams. I didn't think anything of it."

"You wouldn't, darling. Never mind. You just concentrate on the gallery, and I'll do some research of my own."

Bemused, Mark busied himself by wrapping a sublime little Godfrey Miller he had just sold, off his website, to a Sydney buyer. Painted in the late nineteen fifties, it portrayed a gently sloping pasture ending in a grove of trees. Small rectangular daubes of green and yellow paint, vertically arranged and divided by darker, angled lines, created a pixelated appearance, its geometry reminiscent, thought Mark, of Grace Cossington-Smith. Mark basked in the glow of pleasure at nothing more than just having handled the work, and for only a few weeks at that.

Throughout the morning and early afternoon, a smattering of customers came into the gallery, one couple targeting a charming David Strachan landscape they had seen online. Presented in good light, and engaged by Mark's account of Strachan's impeccable training, his critical acclaim—twice winning the Wynne Prize—and his tragic death aged just fifty in a motor vehicle accident, they had happily acquired the painting.

As he farewelled the proud new owners, Mark sensed Linda's agitation. "Time for some lunch?" he asked.

"No way. Have a look at this."

Mark moved around behind Linda who had been working, uninterrupted, on the computer for almost three hours. "What have you found?"

"I've been trying to track down the Greens. I think Cathy had already found nearly everything. And the repetition of material here makes you cross-eyed. But I found a newspaper article from 1997 featuring Sam Green that mentioned that he'd had to cut short his attendance at a government-sponsored business trip to Jakarta because his son had been injured in a car accident."

"Brad Green?"

Linda looked at Mark as if preparing to say something sharp but then thinking better of it. "That's what I'm assuming, Sherlock."

Mark blushed, and Linda continued.

"I searched for newspaper reports of any car accidents in Sydney on the date he left the business trip. There was a serious accident on the Pacific Highway close to Coff's Harbour that involved two cars and in which four young men were injured, the day before the newspaper report of Sam Green having to leave Jakarta."

"And you think Brad Green might have been one of those young men?"

"Could have been, although there aren't any names published. But all four occupants were said to have been taken to the hospital in Coff's Harbour and one of them was said to have required emergency surgery. It doesn't say exactly what was done but it does say that it was 'life-saving' surgery. What could that have been?"

"It might have been for a chest injury; or a ruptured spleen, that would fit. That sort of surgery would require a big left upper quadrant incision. But, I mean, maybe Brad Green was in that accident, maybe he wasn't. And maybe he did undergo emergency surgery for injuries suffered in that accident, maybe he didn't. And maybe it was a ruptured spleen, who knows? That's an awful lot of maybes."

"Sure is. But maybe," Linda looked up at Mark, her eyes smiling, "if we can find out what actually happened on that day in Coff's Harbour hospital, we could rule this possibility out. I don't think this is any more fanciful than your preoccupation with Rachel Blazov."

Chapter 19
Monday, 5 June 2023

The menial tasks lined up for the working week ahead could not diminish Greta's sense of calm and contentment. She had spent a relaxed and, at times, hedonistic weekend in Lisa's company, mostly in Lisa's comfortable and impeccably appointed Paddington apartment.

They had met up, as planned, on the Friday evening so that Greta could hand over what she'd learnt about Angie Richards, and events had unfolded from there in an easy and amorous way. Although Lisa was attracted to conspiracy theories and enjoyed stretching the rules, Greta's life was rooted in evidence and adherence to the law. Yet the two quickly discovered a shared sense of delight in uncovering the truth about all manner of things; and pleasure in the pursuit of that truth.

Over the course of the weekend, their conversation had repeatedly returned to the topic of Angie's painting and Greta was now trying to get a little closer to the investigation into the fire on Reservoir Street. Lisa had already called to tell her about the sharp observation made by one of the team members in Perth about the cigarette lighter. Greta could not, however, find any record of the whereabouts of Detective Inspector Gary Frobisher who had led the investigation into Angie Richards' death.

It was not unusual for senior police people to seek invisibility after retirement. Not infrequently, they'd made a few enemies along the way. But Gary Frobisher had well and truly gone to ground. No one in the current Arson Squad team knew where he was or, at least, no one there was prepared to say how to get hold of him; and none of them had been involved in the Surry Hills fire. By now, Greta knew the story well – she wouldn't be getting any assistance from that team.

From her time in the Major Crime Squad, Greta recalled that Frobisher was one of the senior colleagues about whom there was always some suspicion. She didn't know him personally, but she also knew that he was someone she preferred to avoid; no one to whom she'd ever wanted to owe a favour, just in case those rumours turned out to be true.

Frobisher had been good friends with her own boss back then, Luke Brand. She trusted Luke and understood how blurred the lines could become between those she could trust and those she could not. Luke had risen to become a Detective Inspector in Major Crime but had not been promoted further, at least not yet. She didn't know if that had been his choice, and she hadn't asked. Her own demotion, as she knew it had been, meant she'd had little contact with him for several years. But she still had his phone number, and she gave him a call.

"Luke Brand."

"Hi Luke, It's Greta McCartney, how are you?"

"Good thanks Gret. Nice to hear from you. How're you doing?"

"All good here, Luke. Can I ask you a favour?"

"Sure. Fire away."

"I'm trying to contact Gary Frobisher. Can you point me in the right direction?"

"Why's that?"

"I'm interested in an old arson case. Back in 2010. He was DI on the case, and I've got some new information that I want to check out with him."

"Is Fraud Squad branching out these days?"

Greta could hear the cooling of Luke's tone, perhaps also a hint of mockery. She shut her eyes and continued. "I've checked with Arson – they don't know, and they don't care. You know what it's like for me. I just want to check if Gary had any sense that it wasn't quite the accident they said it was. Then I'll be happy. You know a woman died in that fire."

"What's it got to do with Fraud?"

"It's an unrelated inquiry. A social acquaintance of mine reached out when they found something that might point to a possible motive for homicide. It's vague but, well, not that vague."

"Sounds like it's something for us, Gret, wouldn't you say?"

"Take it from me, Luke. If there's anything in this, I'll be in touch right away."

"Good. You do that and I'll see if Gary wants to be found. If he does, he'll be in touch."

Chapter 20
Tuesday, 6 June 2023

Two emails caught Mark's attention as he sat at his gallery desk and warmed his hands on his cup of tea. The first was from Henry Lew passing on the response from John Brodzky, last surviving child of Horace Brodzky. Still in control of his faculties albeit now at an advanced age, John had agreed that the small painting in question was very much in the style of his late father and that, as far as he could tell, the character on the left was intended to be his father. The painting itself was not one he could recall ever having seen but he had been barely ten years of age at the time indicated on the little painting. As for the other characters in the painting, at that low magnification, none bore resemblance to anyone John knew or could recall.

If the central female figure was intended to have been Rachel Blazov, Mark felt sure that Brodzky's son would have recognised her.

A little disappointed, Mark opened the second, from a New Zealand artist named Denis O'Connor. Mark had drawn a blank on Lorne Etherington's little abstract, connecting with established Australian artist Derek O'Connor to discover yet another skilled exponent of abstraction, but not the maker of the little work in question. Denis was the only other recognised artist with the name "D. O'CONNOR" he could locate, and he'd responded to Mark's inquiry with enthusiasm. His email stated:

Wow! Yes, that's mine, a very early work from 1974. It's prompted a frantic search for records from that time. Where did you find it?

The email went on to describe the technique the artist had used to make it and a little about what he had done in his career since that time. It was a generous, joyous reaction and Mark couldn't wait to tell Lorne that he had identified the artist; to Mark, it felt as if he was reconnecting Lorne with a distant relative that he never knew he had. Without doubt, thought Mark, this was the best part of his job.

Mark's next task was to track down the medical records at Coff's Harbour. The connection between this car accident and their search for the origins of Aresh's painting was a long shot to start with and putting it to bed depended upon extracting information that was a quarter of a century old. As was his experience in most matters IT, the internet proved confusing. He located the public hospital in Coff's Harbour but couldn't be sure that this had even been the place where those car accident victims had been taken back in the nineties. He had no contacts at that hospital and had to hope that Aresh might instead.

*****

"Hi. Fraud Squad. Greta McCartney speaking."

"Greta. This is Gary Frobisher. Luke Brand said you wanted to speak to me."

Greta checked her wristwatch. It was just after eleven thirty am. Just the sound of his voice made her pulse hasten. "Thanks Gary. I am so sorry to disturb you. But you'd be doing me a big favour if you could recall some details about a fire you investigated back in 2010. I'm sure you'll remember it – a young artist named Angie Richards died in that fire. On Reservoir Street, Surry Hills."

"Sure. I remember it well. She was probably drunk or stoned when whatever she was smoking triggered the fire. We were very confident about that. Luke said you had new information that suggested we'd got it wrong. What sort of information was it?"

"It's all a bit vague but I'll tell you what I've got." Greta closed her eyes in concentration and continued. "A journalist acquaintance has heard from another artist from that time, that Richards had told him that she was in a toxic relationship back then. This friend had always wondered if the fire had been intentional – you know, the partner getting rid of her. Did you hear about any trouble Richards had had with her partner at the time?"

"No, there was nothing like that, and we definitely looked for a possible motive. Why didn't that other artist come forward at the time? Seems a bit strange bringing that up now."

"Exactly. That's why the journalist wanted someone to check into the story before she took it too far. She said that other guy's a bit unreliable. Gary, all I need to know is that you were satisfied you'd considered all the angles."

"Fair enough. We did a thorough job. Truly, there's nothing to see here, Greta. If I was you, I'd leave it to Arson, OK?"

"Sure. Thanks Gary. I think this'll probably stop it in its tracks."

"Is that everything?"

Greta pondered Frobisher's question. "Yep. All done. Really appreciate your time. You keep well."

The conversation ended. Greta texted Lisa:

"Can we catch up at Ten William Street tonight? Paddington. Say, at six?"

*****

Aresh had never worked in Coff's Harbour, but he had trained with two of the Consultant Obstetricians now working there and one of them, Gabriela Bernado, was the current Head of Department. She had impressed everyone as a Resident Medical Officer within months of arriving in Sydney from Sao Paulo and had moved quickly and comfortably through the ranks and onto advanced training. A consultant post in Coff's Harbour agreed with her love of the beach and her talent for surfing. Aresh was not surprised to discover that she'd risen to the top in such a plum location.

He contacted her through the switchboard.

"Hi Gaby, how're you doing?"

"I'm sorry, who is this?"

Aresh thought the switchboard person hadn't quite got his name. "It's Aresh Mehta. I'm calling from Perth."

"Aresh! Nice to hear from you. Switch clearly didn't catch your name. How are things going?"

They exchanged updates, quick to reconnect and to fill in the career details of the decade since their last conversation. Aresh savoured his colleague's enduring accent. She had noted his recent appointment in Perth.

"Well done you on the appointment," said Gabriela, "you were always good with your hands. To what do I owe this call?"

Aresh scanned his memory for any double meaning; he was confident that her comment was meant as a compliment, genuine and very surgical, but he doubted himself more and more these days. "Thanks. It's not a super quick story but I'll try to explain. Do you have a few minutes?"

"Sure, I'm intrigued."

"I am keen to find out about an incident back in 1997 when there was car accident near Coff's Harbour and four young men were brought into your hospital with various injuries. I'll send you the newspaper clipping so you'll be able to line up the dates. I appreciate you might not be able to divulge the identify of any of them, but one of the four apparently underwent emergency surgery and, most of all, I am keen to find out about that operation."

"I'm guessing this young man isn't now a patient of yours."

"Gaby, this is not a medical inquiry so much as a search for a possible rapist and murderer. I know that sounds melodramatic, but certain things point to this … potential criminal having been injured in this car accident. As it turns out, the person I'm looking for might have a distinctive laparotomy incision from that time. I don't expect you to give me any name; just that someone did or did not have an emergency op on that date in your hospital."

Aresh could feel the suspicion and disbelief in Gabriela's silence. But he resisted the temptation to say more, waiting for her to respond.

"I don't think anyone here will be all that bothered if I go looking for thirty-year-old case notes. Even if it's a male patient. I'm not sure I'll even find it. But that is one wild story, my friend, and I'm not sure whether to recommend you speak to the police first or to a psychiatrist. Are you sure you're OK?"

"I know, it seems crazy. But we've involved the New South Wales police, and it's more about ruling things out than finding a dangerous killer. It'd be great to tie off this loose end if I could. I know you can't give me his name."

"For an old friend, Aresh, it will be my pleasure. But just mind yourself, won't you? Take it from me, this sounds weird. All that bright Perth sunlight might be affecting you."

They said goodbye, Aresh stewing over feelings of discomfort and anxiety. Asking a long-lost colleague to skate close to privacy constraints on grounds that were undeniably tenuous was bad enough. Stretching the truth about police involvement was almost deceitful. At one level, he hoped that Gaby didn't find anything at all, and certainly nothing that perpetuated this dubious intrigue; it would be better if it could all just disappear. The Australian medical community was close-knit, and he knew that his reputation would not withstand too much of this amateur sleuth routine.

*****

The heavens had opened that afternoon and inner-Sydney traffic was especially heavy. Greta had been struck by the sight of a surging sea of umbrellas, disembodied hemispheres of varying sizes and colours moving along the footpaths and across the roads, as if they were objects being surveilled by a drone from above, each pedestrian represented by their own tracking symbol.

She knew that the weather accounted for Lisa being late but familiar pangs of self-doubt engulfed her, sitting in the bar, as six-fifteen came and went. She ordered a glass of red wine, anticipating the worst, simultaneously chastising herself for being impatient as well as for imagining there'd ever been more to their brief fling than there had. The waiter brought the wine to the table just as Lisa breezed into the bar, poised and striking. They exchanged smiles across the bar, and Lisa glided into the booth, sitting opposite to Greta. "I'm sorry I'm late, it's a mess out there." She leant over the table and kissed Greta on the lips, assured, almost wanton.

"What can I get for you?" asked Greta, a little off balance.

Lisa looked at Greta's glass, and back into Greta's eyes. "One of those would be perfect."

Greta signalled the waiter, pointed to the glass and raised her index finger. His smile signalled that he'd got the message. Greta asked. "How was your day?"

"Pretty good. A few meetings, too many coffees, dozens of emails. Not enough of you."

Greta blushed. "I spoke to that Arson Squad DI, the one involved in the house fire."

"How'd you get hold of him?"

"Actually, he rang me. My friend in Major Crime let him know I had some information about the fire and that was enough for him to call in."

"That didn't take long."

"My thoughts exactly. The fact that he called was probably more important than anything either of us said. If there was nothing to hide in this case, I doubt he'd have been in a hurry to call me. I think he was fishing to see what I knew."

"What did you tell him?"

Greta outlined the brief conversation. "I didn't really lie to him; I just didn't tell him the whole story. He'd have known I was holding back. And I'm certain that if, back then, he'd known about—or even suspected—a possible perpetrator, he'll be unsettled by the news that people are raising the possibility now."

"Unsettled? He's no longer in the force, right?"

"He wouldn't have been working alone so, if they took any shortcuts back then, for whatever reason, they won't want it surfacing again even many years later. I don't know what he'll do now that he knows there's been some new interest in the case. Possibly nothing. He was quick to tell me there was nothing more to it. I think we just need to wait."

"Waiting isn't my style, Greta. You know that." She sipped on her wine only partly obscuring a roguish smile. "I've been brewing an idea for a podcast about this painting. Or maybe even just floating the idea, talking about it as a project that's coming up. A way of bringing all the players out of the shadows. I genuinely think there's more to Angie's painting. But I don't think we are going to get the sort of penetration we need with the information we've currently got."

Greta finished her glass of wine. "You're probably right about getting to the truth. I don't think it's going to be easy. You know, if the Arson Squad cut short that investigation …"

"Or intentionally overlooked evidence" Lisa interjected.

Greta retained a neutral expression. "What I'm saying is that they're not going to rush to help us. And there'll still be people—maybe like Gary Frobisher—who will be keen to keep a lid on it all."

"I'm prepared to poke that bear. There's a crime in here somewhere, Greta, and my friend was the victim. I want to find out who did it. I want us to find out."

Chapter 21
Wednesday, 7 June 2023

Aresh dried the last of the cutlery and replaced it in the kitchen drawer. He'd kept dinner simple, as usual, his mind still re-living the events of a challenging afternoon. He'd been called to labour ward to assist an obstetric colleague confronted by a massive post-partum haemorrhage in a woman delivering her fifth baby. There'd been no time to transfer the woman for radiological intervention; only emergency hysterectomy would save her life.

Operating in these circumstances was technically demanding, bordering on heroic. There was equal need for speed and calm, for decisive action and absolute precision. The successful outcome for their patient had been gratifying, as was the heartfelt appreciation of his colleague. But he had felt rattled, as always, by the proximity of death and the knowledge that these scenarios—and the expectation that he would be there to deal with them—would accompany him throughout his career.

He wanted to call Cathy, but she had made it clear she was not interested in any communication all, at least until after her exams. Aresh was in uneasy territory, conscious of the awkward state of their relationship and of the need for him to be patient while she was under such intense pressure. When his phone rang, just after eight pm, his chest reacted with unexpected anticipation; the "02" prefix on the mobile phone screen caught him by surprise. The accent on the other end of the call made him smile.

"Gaby, this is late for you."

"When did you think I would get around to looking up old case notes, in the middle of a caesarean?"

"Alright then. So, I gather you've tracked down the case in question."

"I sure have. I checked that date and our very old theatre records are saved on a strange thing called "microfiche". Have you ever heard of them?"

"No, I have no idea what that is. Sounds weird."

Gaby explained the old technology, plastic sheets of photocopied notes, shrunken in size but made legible when magnified by their purpose-specific projector. It had been a nightmare for Gaby to navigate, but the records had been clear.

"There was an emergency laparotomy on that night, Friday May ninth. The surgeon was a Mr Bennett and the anaesthetist a Dr Chan. The assistant was 'J. Golding' and they performed a splenectomy and repair of ruptured jejunum via a left upper paramedian incision."

Aresh appreciated the pause, as if prompting him to ask more. "That's incredible, Gaby. That actually fits with what we believe."

"Well, thanks for nothing my friend. Now I have the name of this patient in front of me, and you're telling me he might have been a rapist or a murderer. Do *you* at least have some idea who this person might be?"

"Yes. We do have a possible name. And this new information makes it more likely that he is the one we're after. So, you've really helped us."

"Oh, look at this," said Gaby, as if in mock surprise. "He must have been going on holiday for his birthday." Gaby stopped for a second and then continued, emphasising each word. "He'd have turned nineteen that Sunday. How about that?"

Aresh understood Gaby's intention. A quick calculation and the patient's date of birth was set – May 11th, 1978. "Thanks Gaby, you've been amazing. I'll let you know how all this pans out, OK?"

As soon as the call ended, Aresh googled Brad Green. Although he was nowhere near as proficient at this as were most of his peers, he was able to quickly establish that Brad Green was born in 1978. He recalled that Cathy had already found out quite a bit about Brad Green and knew that his exact date of birth was close at hand. He messaged Mark Lewis:

"Are you free to speak?"

Chapter 22
Thursday, 8 June 2023

The Perth crew assembled at Beaufort Gallery just before five thirty pm. Each of them had found good excuses to make the meeting. Lisa and Greta dialled in spot on time; Lisa introduced Greta and Aresh brought them up to speed with his inquiries into the Coff's Harbour accident.

"Pardon my uncertainty," asked Lisa, "but can you just reassure me that this surgical incision is as significant as you seem to believe? I mean, people are having operations all the time, aren't they? I feel like we're pinning a lot of weight on this."

Mark responded. "Lisa, I think we can be crystal clear about this. That is an uncommon incision at the best of times, reserved for a very limited range of procedures and situations. And it is especially uncommon in an adolescent."

"We know from newspaper reports that Brad Green was involved in a car accident that weekend and the date of birth of the Coff's Harbour patient lines up exactly," said Aresh, glancing at Linda who had established that fact days earlier. "It was Brad Green who had that operation on that night, I have no doubt. I think Angie's painting identified her attacker in multiple ways—the surgical scar, the little painting on the study wall, the mop of dark hair, the lighter maybe. For all we know, the entire study looks exactly as she painted it."

"Is this enough to go to New South Wales police?" asked Helen.

Greta answered. "There's a chance—unfortunately—that the original investigation was cut short, so I'm not sure who exactly I can trust. I'm in Fraud, you know, not Major Crime, and there's a definite pecking order. It's not that everyone is crooked, not at all. But no one will be keen to dig too deeply into past investigations. There'd have to be a solid reason to do that."

"More solid than rape and murder?" asked Olivia.

"You might be surprised," said Greta looking straight at the camera.

Lisa spoke next. "I think what Greta is saying is that whoever committed the original crime will clearly still want to escape attention. We are more and more confident that police interfered in some way with the original investigation, and those police will have equally little interest in the matter being brought up again. I have no doubt that there's a crime and a cover-up in all this and that the people involved were people of considerable influence."

"And might still be," added Greta. "I've spoken to the guy who investigated the fire and he wouldn't give me anything. I've got no pull at all with the people in Major Crime. And I'm not authorised to approach Brad Green. If I break ranks on this, I'll alert exactly the people we're trying to expose."

"Why don't you speak to Brad Green directly?" Mark asked. "I mean you, Lisa."

"I'd love to," said Lisa.

"I wouldn't recommend that either," said Greta. "I think we still need to figure out more about what took place. Find out what we still don't know."

"I remember that Angie was doing quite well painting portraits," said Lisa, "so it's not crazy to suggest that she'd been engaged to do a portrait in the Green household. I think we should be working on the assumption that the rape scene *is* real, and that Brad Green *is* the rapist. What I don't know is whether he knew about this painting. Or even how he could have. I saw the exhibition at Galerie Strauss and it's a long time ago, but I'm completely certain this work was not there. I'd have remembered seeing Angie in a painting, that's for sure."

"The rape scene is dated January, and the exhibition was held in June," Pat said as if thinking out loud. "Angie left the painting for Lisa at the same time the exhibition opened, and she was dead within forty-eight hours."

They all waited for Pat to make his point.

"Something about that exhibition triggered her murder," he continued. "It's as if Angie suddenly knew that the painting was a liability, that Green somehow knew about its' existence—or at least suspected it—and that Green would want to find it and get rid of it."

"But he couldn't have found the painting in Angie's apartment, because it was in Coogee at our place. Maybe he set fire to the studio in case he'd missed it," Lisa suggested.

"More likely to disguise the method of murder, I'm afraid," said Greta in a sober tone. "I think the decision to set fire to the apartment was a measured one. Maybe Green had gone to the apartment to confront Angie, possibly to find and destroy a painting he suspected she'd painted, but things got out of hand. He murdered her or hurt her badly and then needed some assistance. He probably called someone he knew to get help. And setting fire to the place, ensuring it was a fierce fire, to me that suggests professional advice."

"But he left the lighter there," said Pat. "And that makes me think Green did it on his own. A professional would not have left that behind."

"I'm not so sure," said Greta. "Even though the lighter might have linked the fire back to Green and the painting, the police later used the lighter to implicate Angie as the cause of the fire. If it wasn't Angie's, Green might well have left it behind by mistake. But he might also have done so on purpose. I doubt Green could have figured that out for himself. I suspect he was told to leave it behind."

"Greta, are you saying that it might have been police who helped Green back then?" asked Mark.

"It's possible, I'm afraid."

"So, Lisa speaking to Brad Green will just alert them all?"

"At this stage, Mark, that's what worries me. I think it might draw attention to Lisa—and to all of us I suppose—making us the targets. In any event, I suspect that some of the people who I assume helped him back then already know that there are new rumours circulating about the possibility of Angie being murdered. I'd be surprised if the ex-Arson Squad DI I spoke to hasn't already shared our conversation with other people."

For a few seconds there was silence, Mark trying to fathom the high stakes with which they were all now dealing.

"Lisa has an idea to try and provoke Green, to disrupt his sense of control, and to force him and whoever's been helping him do something they wouldn't otherwise do. Something that the Arson Squad can't easily close down. Left to their own devices, much of the police force, even perfectly good people, would be happy leaving things be."

Greta looked towards Lisa as if cuing her to speak. "My plan," said Lisa, "is to pursue this as a podcast. I can do this in stages because my current show still has several weeks to run. And the one after that is well under production. What I plan to do is to start promoting a new show, a true crime investigation, and to provide enough information to unnerve Brad Green. Obviously, I'll not refer to him by name but, say, as a 'prominent Sydney business personality'. I'll float the idea that we're looking into the death of a rising star of Australian art in a house fire. I'll talk about new evidence that suggests the investigation into her death failed to seriously consider the possibility of murder."

"How will this reach Brad Green? Or the Arson Squad team?" asked Pat. "And what will Angie's family think if they get wind of this?"

"I'll make sure the Arson Squad hear about it straight away," said Greta. "I'll tell them I listen to Lisa's podcast. I mean, if I don't come forward with this, they'll assume I'm involved, given that I've already spoken to them about the case. Me bringing up the planned podcast with them without delay will make some sense to them, as if I'm washing my hands of my involvement."

"And to be honest," said Lisa, "I'd really like Angie's family to contact me. They might form an important part of the subsequent podcast. I bet they've never been totally convinced about the cause of her death either."

"And Green? He's the one who has the most to lose here." Pat sounded concerned. "How will you make sure he knows?"

"I've thought about that, Pat. I'm going to send him an anonymous note," said Lisa. "It'll be clean so no one will be able to trace it back to me. But it will be plain speaking: 'You raped and murdered Angie Richards. There is evidence. Your time is running out.' That sort of thing." The crew in Perth remained silent. "Well, that's the plan," Lisa concluded.

Greta spoke next. "There's a chance this will have no impact. Maybe they'll just hold the line and wait to see whether there's any substance to Lisa's claims. In some respects, that would be the safest thing for them to do. But I imagine Brad Green is going to be hard to keep under control. I'm not sure who else knows about the rape but I'm confident now that he believed that there was an incriminating painting. Which he's never seen and cannot be sure doesn't still exist. I'm sure this is going to excite a reaction from him at least."

Pat persevered. "You two are both putting yourselves at some sort of risk, aren't you? I mean, the Arson Squad know about Greta's interest. And the podcast promo will tell them about you, Lisa. If Greta's right that Green accessed professional advice on the night of the fire, surely he still has some sort of access today? Have you thought it all through? We can't bring Angie back to life, you know. Please, let's not have any more casualties on account of this painting."

"That's a good point Pat. I recognise the risks for me and Lisa and I'm putting some protection in place. Most importantly, we have a plan to escalate the pressure on Green, if we have to. Ultimately, we can use the painting itself—or the threat of it—to expose him. I think we're piecing together what really happened that night. And that we can establish the truth for everyone to see."

It was dark outside the gallery as the meeting ended. Mark said goodbye and the visitors exited the gallery. Linda stood up and approached Angie's painting and asked Mark, "Where are you going to keep this one safe?"

Chapter 23
Friday, 9 June 2023

Lisa uploaded her latest podcast interview along with the short introductory promo for her planned true crime story just after eleven am. She texted Greta to let her know and sat back in her office chair happy that this was the right thing to do. She had posted the anonymous letter to Brad Green, marked "Private and Confidential" the previous evening and expected he would receive it today.

She'd packed a suitcase at Greta's instruction; she would be moving in with her after work and staying at her place over the weekend. She doubted that the precaution was necessary, but she fancied being in close contact with Greta for the next few days, so she hadn't resisted. On all accounts, she was excited.

*****

Greta waited until exactly four thirty to make the call to her former Major Crime colleague. "Luke, it's Greta McCartney again. Sorry to bother you."

"No worries, Greta. What's up?"

"It's about that fire I called you about on Monday. Thanks for getting Frobisher to call me. He had nothing to add, but the person who involved me in the first place has obviously taken it further."

"Oh yes. What's happened?"

"There's a podcaster I listen to, and she's just uploaded her latest episode at the very end of which she's made clear reference to an upcoming story she intends to run which is going to be all about a fire in which a young woman died. And how a prominent local businessperson is somehow going to be implicated. I'm certain it's the same matter I asked you about. Honestly, I know this looks like I'm involved, but I have no idea about the victim and even less about this businessperson. Luke, I'm not somehow trying to resurrect my career by solving made-up crimes. I know where I stand." Greta took a breath and then continued. "You might want to let Frobisher know. I'm sure you can imagine that I'm regretting speaking to you both about this."

"What's the name of the podcast?"

Greta could hear the ice in Luke Brand's voice. "The Female Voice. The podcaster's name is Lisa Dimopoulos. She's based here in Sydney."

"Something tells me this is going to be a shitstorm. Is there anything else you should be telling me?"

"Nothing Luke. That's what I know."

"See you later McCartney," and he hung up.

Luke's irritation was palpable. Greta knew he would be sharing this new information with the Arson Squad some time very soon. If that Squad harboured any residual link back to Frobisher—or whoever else had been involved in the investigation into Angie's death—this new information would be of intense interest to them. The people with most to hide would be alerted with little delay. The tempo was picking up. Greta felt a thrill.

*****

Helen O'Beirne had been in the art business long enough to know all of the established gallerists and auction personnel in every major Australian city. Of course, new galleries appeared all the time and her contacts inside the system were, like her, advancing in age. But Judith Strauss and her Woollahra gallery had been a fixture on the Sydney art scene for most of the time Helen and Pat had been an equivalent fixture in the Perth art scene. Although Galerie Strauss had closed eight years ago, Judith's number remained in Helen's list of contacts.

"Hi Judith, it's Helen O'Beirne in Perth. How are you doing?"

"I'm doing well for an old girl, Helen. How are you? And to what do I owe the pleasure of this call?"

Helen appreciated the cultured, almost upper crust English twang of Judith's accent. She recalled cringing at what she had initially regarded as a snobby affectation amongst so many people in art circles. But she'd got to know many of them well enough to know that it counted for very little. Judith, in particular, had always been honest and open in her dealings with Helen, happy to share important information about the provenance of artworks of mutual interest, and unguarded in her assessment of people and businesses with whom she had traded.

The two women chatted, still at ease with each other, recalling a sad conversation when Judith had lost her husband of more than thirty years; and their mutual commiserations not long after that, in 2015, shortly after Galerie Strauss had closed. They'd both endured the financial struggles that had beset large swathes of the Australian art gallery industry from about 2010, Judith opting to retire, Helen and Pat having survived and now forging ahead. Helen brought their reminiscing to a close.

"I have come across a painting made in 2010 by an artist named Angie Richards who you represented. I know that she died in a house fire, and I'm told you were holding an exhibition of her works when she died, but I can't find out very much more about her or that exhibition. I was hoping you could help me."

"Oh yes. That was so awful. Apparently, she was … under the influence … when she accidentally set fire to her studio and apartment. We'd opened the show a few nights earlier and there was a lot of interest in them. But the works were rather confronting and only a few had sold before she died. We ended up having to return the rest of them to her parents a month or two later because the market for her work disappeared overnight. She was well-trained and a very, very good painter. It was tragic."

"I suppose the painting I've got must have been one of those that sold," Helen lied, biting her lip. "It's a pretty violent image, to be honest."

"They all were, as I recall. Murder and self-harm, suffering and the like. Not ones you'd want to remember in too much detail if you could help it."

"Do you still have a list of the works in that exhibition? And which ones were sold? I am keen to place the work properly for the owners."

"Absolutely, my dear. I've kept records of everything we ever handled. I'll fish it out this afternoon and give you a call."

"I'll text you through my email as well, Judith. It's so nice of you to help out."

"Can you send me an image of your painting? I'd love to remind myself of that initial impression."

"Let me check with the owner first. They're a little iffy about who sees what they've got, but I think they'll be OK. Thanks again for your help."

Helen exhaled slowly after she put the phone down. She owed it to Judith—and to herself—to unravel the lies she'd just spun as soon as it was safe.

*****

Brad Green breezed into his central city offices just before midday. He'd had an enjoyable morning – a late coffee with his girlfriend, Loretta, after an extended workout in the local gym. He needed to clear his desk of a few documents before a business lunch in Darlinghurst with a couple of potential new investors trying to gain a foothold in the seemingly never-ending Sydney real estate goldmine. And then he and Loretta were off to the family beach house in Palm Beach for the long weekend. Life was good and he didn't doubt that he was a fortunate man.

His Office Manager, Maddy, greeted him with a stern look. "The Billinghurst contract needs to be counter-signed and there are minutes of the last two board meetings that you still need to review and sign. Dominic is getting a little tetchy about them."

Brad knew that look and understood that he couldn't defer these duties any longer. Other people had, of course, already made the important decisions, and any critical actions would have been put in place. But he still held executive authority inside Green Enterprises and he knew these delays generated lots of irritation. He entered his office with its breath taking view of the bridge and harbour. And with its small but select display of paintings and sculptures, each a little treasure of Australian art in its own right, which he and his father had accumulated over the years.

A manila folder contained the documents for his perusal and signature; he sat and signed them, where indicated, not bothering to read what he knew would be in perfect order and were, he conceded, of no interest to him. A letter marked "Private and Confidential" had been opened with a letter-opener but had not been read; he withdrew the single sheet of paper and unfolded it.

As Brad read the message, he broke out in intense perspiration. He felt dazed and angry. The note was an unambiguous threat, but it was the absence of any demand that he found especially terrifying. Someone knew what had happened. But who could it be? What evidence did they have? What did they want from him? And why now? "Those fucking police," he said to himself, but still out loud.

He knew who he had to call but he needed to calm down. He put the anonymous letter in his pocket, found a gym towel in one of the cupboards and wiped the perspiration off his face and neck. He grabbed his second phone from inside the top drawer of his desk, disconnected it from its charger and slipped it into his jacket pocket. He headed out of the office with a cursory goodbye to the

Office Manager but, just as the elevator arrived, turned back into the office and said, "Maddy, I've signed the documents. Could you cancel today's lunch? Something's just cropped up."

*****

Brad needed absolute privacy and his car was the best place. He slid into his brand-new Tesla and dialled Ray Chalmers. He emerged into traffic on Macquarie Street, heading north, grateful that the full onslaught of the Friday afternoon traffic was still an hour or two away. Chalmers answered and Brad got quickly to the point.

"I've just received an anonymous letter that says that they have evidence that I raped and murdered that artist. They don't identify themselves and they don't make any demands. All they say is that my time is running out. This has got to be someone from the force, don't you think? No one else knows about the fire but the police." He was indicating right at the M1, heading towards his home, his actions unconscious. "Honestly, Ray, you've got to help me."

"I hear you, Bradley. I can't talk right now. Have you got that anonymous note with you?"

"Yes, I've got it here." He patted his jacket as if Chalmers could see him.

"Don't touch it again, OK? Just leave it where it is. I'll call you back in a few minutes."

The Tesla issued a mildly worded warning about his speed and Brad eased off the accelerator trying to gather his thoughts. 'We know about the rape and murder' it had said. He dwelt on that for a moment. How did they know about the rape? Not that it had been rape, the teasing bitch. And he'd destroyed the only evidence he knew there'd been. And the fire would surely have taken care of anything else.

Perhaps she'd told someone about them, about all of it before the fire – he'd always wondered if she had. But why would they only bring it up now? In any event, whatever they had on him might prove embarrassing, even humiliating. But, it was unlikely to be anything that would hold up in court. He couldn't figure it out. Even if someone knew about their relationship, how had they made a connection to the fire? Hadn't the evidence been watertight?

Brad's thoughts were in disarray, tumbling and flailing in a maelstrom of fear and confusion, grasping at flimsy threads, unable to arrest his fall. The more he thought about it, the more he believed that the police had to be responsible. And that there would be another payoff waiting to be solicited. It would all turn out to be about money.

He took the slip road on the left for Moore Park Road. His phone rang. It was Ray Chalmers, and his voice was clear and calm.

"Are you alone Bradley?"

Green hated the condescension in Chalmers' tone and his slow, deliberate tempo, but he had no choice other than to put up with it. "Yes, I'm in my car and I'm on my own."

"I think you and I need to catch up, Bradley. Face to face. Something's obviously cropped up and we need to figure out what that might be. This is kind of pressing, so it'd be good if we can get together this weekend. You haven't got anything more important planned, have you?"

Expletives crossed Brad's mind like a machine gun blast. His weekend away with Loretta was now in tatters and this change of plans was going to be hard to explain to her. What made him feel most alarmed, however, was his reliance, once again, on this fiend of a man. He knew that he had no choice but to comply. "Just tell me where and when, and I'll be there."

*****

Gary Frobisher scanned his apartment. He had rented it for years, since shortly before his retirement, an exemplary tenant from the outset. The cost of renting it had always been comfortably outstripped by the income earned from letting out his own, much larger house in Ashfield. Now, the time to find a new place to live had arrived, much as he had always suspected it one day would. He had planned his retirement carefully, aware that the choices he'd made that had financed it so comfortably might later return to haunt him. That time had come.

He had only just finished a call from Luke Brand advising him of the impending true crime podcast about the Surry Hills fire, complete with information that made it clear that the podcaster had at least some important facts right, when Ray Chalmers called. That was a rare event indeed but Chalmers' account of the anonymous threat to Brad Green seemed to Frobisher like perfectly reasonable grounds for Chalmers to break the prolonged silence between the two former colleagues.

And, thought Frobisher, whoever had put this bomb under Brad Green's lazy arse, will be the same person feeding the podcaster the story. But why now?

"You recall that Green told us he was worried the girl had a painting that exposed his relationship with her."

"That implied he'd raped her," Frobisher interjected.

"Green never looked at it that way, you will recall, and was always more anxious that his wife and family would find out. Anyway, that was why he'd gone to Reservoir Street that night, to find a painting," said Chalmers.

"I recall it all, Ray. He told us that he couldn't find it and we certainly never saw any evidence that there'd ever been a painting. Maybe that's what's surfaced after all these years."

"They obviously believe that there was a rape *and* a murder. I don't know how, just yet. Even if there was a painting, it could only point to rape. I suspect they are guessing she was murdered. So, the question is why haven't they gone to the police? That's what really bothers me, Gary."

"Perhaps they believe the force won't look into it because the original investigation was fixed? Maybe that's why they haven't taken it back to the police." As he thought out loud, Gary pictured Greta McCartney. He'd suspected straight away that her story was dodgy; now he was sure that she was involved, possibly even calling the shots. And he understood she'd know enough about his reputation to have put two and two together.

"I agree. There's no doubt they think there was a cover-up. Whatever new piece of information has dragged up this stinking corpse, it will definitely be recent. They won't have been sitting on it for more than ten years, you can be sure of that. I reckon they might have taken it to the force first up, but someone inside has warned them off, made it clear not to expect any help from the police. So, now they're ruffling Green's feathers and waiting to see what happens. I need to know who that person is on the inside – who would they have taken this to?"

"Major Crime or Arson, Ray. Which of them liked us the least?"

"Or used us the most. I'll have to do some digging. But you've still got mates in both areas, so you ask around as well. I'll need to close this down quickly. Green is a total dickhead, and I don't trust him to keep his cool. Get onto it today. Please."

"I'm moving as you speak, Ray."

Frobisher switched off the phone. Ray Chalmers had seriously violent connections and Gary had no doubt that he would use those connections to eliminate anyone he suspected might expose his history of corruption and crime. Gary had not told Chalmers about Greta McCartney in large part to protect her – he wasn't interested in any more violence occurring on his account. He was also protecting himself; Chalmer's search for that inside source would buy Frobisher time. Time to disappear.

*****

Helen had spent the day in their Nedlands gallery, mostly on the phone as she contacted clients whose works she was soliciting for the November sale. It was still months away, but securing major pieces was critical for the overall standing of the sale; spirited bidding on the top-flight pieces often raised the tenor of the auction and lifted prices all round. But extracting these works from their owners' homes and collections required perseverance and diplomacy in equal portions. This was her domain, not Pat's.

Helen detested getting stuck in traffic, so she was already in her car and heading home when Judith Strauss rang her. "Did you get my email?"

"Sorry Judith, I've just left the gallery and missed it. Did you find the exhibition catalogue?"

"Yes, and I've got images of all the pieces in it. There were ten paintings and four drawings, mostly studies for the paintings. It's a ghoulish collection but she really was talented. I've got the prices as well, but only two paintings and one drawing were sold, so I'm not sure you can attribute too much weight to those prices. As I said, I expect you'll be holding one of those two that sold. I've also sent through her first exhibition with us, the year before. Much less confronting and they sold quite nicely. It's all in the email."

Helen had made her way down Stirling Highway, past the University of Western Australia, with its stately Winthrop Hall dominating the administrative heart of the campus to her right and its residential colleges to her left. Her car curved along Mounts Bay Road, Crawley's grand apartments and then Kings' Park rising steeply on one side and the broad expanse of the Swan River, still and flat on a windless winter afternoon, on the other. "Thanks so much, Judith. I'll look at the emails this evening and I'll be in touch. Have a lovely weekend."

Helen took the slip road onto the freeway heading south, pleased that she had beaten the rush hour and excited to see the images that her colleague had sent through. She sensed that the answer to their mystery was close at hand.

*****

It was difficult for Greta to separate the various causes of her excitement. She had left work earlier than usual to prepare her place for Lisa's visit, keen to have things looking spick and span and anxious to start the preparations for dinner. Her unpretentious semi-detached house was presentable but nothing like Lisa's smartly appointed apartment; Greta's lifelong insecurities hovered beside her, she recognised, like an awkward relative at a family celebration.

Her family had raised their collective eyebrows when she purchased the insanely expensive property over fifteen years ago. Having been raised in Cronulla, Greta's decision to buy in Bondi was greeted with a mixture of surprise and hurt. More of that followed in short order when she came out. To a conservative, Catholic family, the double-hit of having a lesbian in the family and a daughter living in the midst of a distinctly non-Catholic part of their city was hard to accept. Greta appreciated that, in turn, she had also struggled to fully accept herself and that moving well away from her roots was a part of undertaking that process.

As it turned out, the neighbours with whom she shared a common wall were exactly what her parents had supposed – a Jewish family complete with loud Friday night dinners and an unpredictable but relentless succession of crowded celebrations sprinkled throughout the year. The Liebs had been friendly to the point of over-sharing; and they'd been unmoved by Greta's sexual orientation. As Greta's siblings, at least, began to relax about their policewoman sister and her choices, so her entire family had relaxed about the Liebs and about the Eastern Suburbs as a whole.

Yet, as Greta set the table and fussed over her choice of wine for dinner, doubts about her own worthiness ever present, there was another source of her unease. In her desire to help and impress Lisa, she knew that she was playing with fire. At a professional level, she was comfortable with the plan to expose Brad Green and whoever inside the force had assisted him. At a personal level, however, the prospect remained that people with influence and hostile connections might target Lisa. Greta could look after herself – but could she look after Lisa?

It was this combination of apprehension and the powerful urge to protect Lisa, now mixed with the simple excitement of having her very new girlfriend spend dinner and the weekend with her, that Greta found novel but distracting.

She settled on the Taittinger, which was cooling in the fridge, but kept the Bin 389 on the sideboard in reserve. She peered out of the front window, unconsciously scanning Midelton Road, tranquil at this time of day, for anything out of the ordinary, before pulling the curtains shut. She turned the outside light on and returned to the kitchen to check on the progress of her eggplant parmigiana.

*****

Helen O'Beirne entered her Salter Point home, situated opposite parkland and the Canning River. It would be just her and Pat for dinner and she hadn't made any plans. Perhaps they'd go out for a meal; or maybe settle for take-away. All she could think about was looking at Judith Strauss's email.

In her study, she turned on her computer. As it booted up, she looked up at the wall above her desk. Their painting of a lone explorer standing windswept in a hostile, snowbound landscape—one of Sydney Nolan's seminal series of works from the nineteen sixties honouring Antarctic exploration—took her attention and, as it always did, calmed her. Nolan had portrayed the explorer as vulnerable and alone, yet simultaneously defiant and single-minded.

She opened Outlook and Judith's email was at the top.

Each of the fourteen images had been attached separately. She first looked at the paintings, starting with those that had not been purchased. The style and subject matter were consistent throughout, including local Sydney references in the images and in their titles. Not surprisingly, none of the ten paintings Judith had sent was the one now sitting in Mark Lewis's gallery.

The first image of a drawing she looked at was a study for the painting in the exhibition that depicted a murder, a confronting stabbing, the victim's pale face portraying his agonal surprise; Helen revisited the equivalent painting, admiring the way that the artist had captured the horror and pain of the attack without descending into gory detail. Likewise, the second drawing, a car accident inflicting evidently fatal injury to the driver and sole occupant, could be paired to one of the paintings. And the third, both drawing and painting, depicted a shooting, an armed robbery that appeared to have gone horribly wrong. In each work, Helen recognised the formal groupings of the characters, as if they were actors in these grim scenes, as well as their distinctive, languid hand gestures in the style adopted by Horace Brodzky and, in turn, derived from Piero Della Francesca.

The fourth drawing was simply entitled "Study". Helen recognised the scene immediately although there was no matching painting listed in this exhibition. It was a rape in an office, the same desk as in Angie's painting, but drawn from a position that was closer to both victim and assailant than in Angie's painting of the same scene. To the left, on the wall, there was the left half only of the Brodzky painting, capturing only the balding, masked man facing towards the drawing's edge, away from the assault. But it was definitely part of the same little painting captured on the same study wall.

The proximity of the drawing to the victim and attacker meant that only the torso of the rapist had been depicted, his neck and face severed by the drawing's upper limit. But his abdomen bore a clear surgical scar identical to the one in the painting.

The victim in this version was wearing the mask, her identity obscured. Helen pondered Angie's intention by including this drawing in the exhibition but not its matching oil. And why had she disguised herself in the drawing but not in the painting? Would Angie have anticipated that Brad Green would attend the exhibition? Perhaps Green was a regular in the Sydney gallery scene. Or possibly even a collector. If he had seen the drawing, that surgical scar would have horrified him.

Helen picked up her phone and rang her former colleague.

"Judith, sorry to call you so late. It's Helen again."

"Think nothing of it. Have you identified the work you have?"

"Yes, sort of. But the painting I have here was the pair to the drawing entitled "Study", the rape scene in an office. This painting obviously didn't make it to the exhibition."

Judith was silent for a minute before she said, "I definitely didn't see a matching work in oil for that drawing. I wonder why she didn't include it. Are you sure it's by Angie? I'd love to see an image of it."

"And I'd love to know who bought the drawing, Judith. I think whoever did might be quite interested in having this one as well, don't you?"

"Maybe they would, but I don't really recall who bought it. It's been well over ten years. I'll have a look again at the image and see if it prompts any old memories."

"Just one more question, and then I'll give you a break."

Judith chuckled, and Helen continued. "You might never have heard of him, but was the businessman Brad Green a collector back in those days? Does his name ring a bell?"

"Of course, yes, I remember. Bradley was a regular visitor to the gallery, and he bought several pieces from me – and from other galleries, I'm told. His father was a major collector for a while here. The old man had a good eye and was happy to buy the best stuff. And, yes, that's right!"

Helen could almost hear Judith's thoughts falling into place.

"It was definitely Brad Green who bought that drawing. He came to the opening. I remember now. And literally snatched it off the wall, insisting he have it there and then. It wasn't framed, you know. We hadn't framed any of the drawings, just had them pinned to cardboard. And he took it home, board and all. We wanted it to stay for the whole exhibition, of course. Yes, I remember that now very clearly." Judith caught her breath. "Why do you ask about Bradley Green?"

"Are you near a computer?"

"Yes …"

"I'll send you an image of the painting I have. Will you call me as soon as you have it?"

*****

Ray Chalmers sipped on his whiskey. He was partial to Irish single malt and was attached to his after-dinner routine of a large tumbler, one third filled with Bushmills sixteen-year-old whiskey, which he sipped in his study as he listened to some classical music. He preferred concerti to symphonies. Mozart's clarinet concerto—a rare recording by Benny Goodman—was playing, its soothing, second movement almost over; for once, it had failed to settle his agitation.

He retraced the afternoon's events. His conversation with Gary Frobisher had left him feeling ill at ease; he had sensed that Frobisher wasn't telling him the whole truth. He'd immediately called Paul Lenzo, a senior member of the Arson

Squad, telling him that news was trickling through that an old case might be opened again and asking Paul if he'd heard anything about it.

Lenzo had said "no" but had later called Chalmers back with the news that they'd only just heard that a podcaster was threatening to expose a Sydney businessman for the rape and murder of the artist who'd died in the 2010 fire on Reservoir Street. Lenzo hadn't been involved in that fire investigation, but he owed his current position and standing to Ray Chalmers, reward for Lenzo's less than scrupulous work—at Chalmers' direction—while he had been working in the Drug Squad. That had been challenging work, at times frightening, and Paul had been only too happy to exchange favours with his imposing superior officer to help him get out of that area. And the debt had never really disappeared.

Since Lenzo's call, Chalmers had been unable to raise Gary Frobisher. As he swirled the last drops of his whiskey around his glass, he concluded that Frobisher had chosen to disappear. In so choosing, the reality of the threat from this unexpected interest in the Surry Hills fire was confirmed in Chalmers' mind, loud and clear. That he would now have to respond to the threat this all posed to him without his capable colleague to help him heightened his unease.

The concerto's final movement was rising to its delicate, understated climax. Chalmers knew Frobisher could be trusted to remain invisible and silent. Just the same, he could picture multiple threats rising before his eyes, one after the other, like the finale of a fireworks display; the damned journalist; the person who'd found the new information – whatever that was; someone inside the force who believed the fire investigation had been cut short; and Brad Green himself.

He had an idea how he could deal with two of those threats in one move. His next call was to Danny "Nails" Finnerty, head of the Assassins motorcycle club.

Chapter 24
Saturday, 10 June 2023

By the time Brad Green had reached the turn-off to Ray Chalmers' Mulgoa property on the very edge of the Blue Mountains National Park, he had adjusted to driving Loretta's Toyota. Chalmers had warned him off driving his Tesla; on this occasion, a lower profile was in order. He felt like he'd been in the car for hours when he finally eased his way the up the private road to which he'd been directed. Chalmers' house, a mansion, was easily located on the left, twelve hundred metres from the turn-off. Green parked, exhaled slowly and headed towards the front door.

"Glad you could make it, Brad. It seems there is more to this matter than you might be aware. Do you know about the podcast?"

Blood drained from Green's face. "Nothing at all. What's that about?"

Chalmers ushered Green into his home. The land, an empty block, had been purchased outright with the proceeds of his assistance to the Green family back in 2010. They sat in comfortable lounge chairs and Chalmers offered tea and biscuits. Brad could not detect the presence of anyone else in the house.

"Did you bring the anonymous note?"

Green reached into his jacket pocket and retrieved the envelope, handing it over to Chalmers like a traffic infringement notice to an exasperated parent. Chalmers glanced at the note before placing it in his own pocket.

"It seems some information must have surfaced that links you to both rape and murder. You destroyed the drawing from that exhibition, didn't you?"

"Of course. I did that before I went to her studio."

"Did you keep a copy, perhaps?"

"Absolutely not," Green said, a little more forcefully than he had intended.

Chalmers held out both hands, palms downwards, as if urging Brad to lower his voice. "But the gallery will have kept an electronic copy, won't they? Which gallery was it, anyway?"

"Galerie Strauss, but they closed down quite a few years back. And even if they had kept a copy, why would that come up now? She didn't really identify me in that drawing, anyway. It was mainly a warning to me, or a threat. The whole thing was set up to make me believe that there was a painting of …. well, an equivalent painting. That's what I was looking for." Brad looked away from Chalmers and glared. "And it wasn't bloody rape, either."

"Yes, Bradley, I know all that. Let's stay calm." Chalmers smiled, equal parts reassurance and menace. "Perhaps that painting did exist and has surfaced now. And it identifies you. Or perhaps there's some other information. What is now clear is that a Sydney podcaster is about to go public with a true crime … show … that threatens to expose a prominent Sydney business identity. I think you can expect this to become very difficult for you."

Brad Green flushed with anger. "It's not going to be all that good for you either, Ray. I mean, if I go down, how will I keep you out of it? Can't we stop them? Do they really have anything solid? And, if they do, why haven't they involved the police?"

Chalmers remained cool, his expression inscrutable. After a long pause, he said, "It's a woman, actually. This podcaster. Her name is Lisa Dimopoulos. And I think you should meet with her, Bradley, somewhere neutral. If it's not you she is about to expose, she'll be fascinated to understand why you want to meet with her. Maybe there's another podcast for her in this. And, if you are the person she is about to expose, she won't be able to resist the chance to interview the killer."

Brad closed his eyes at Chalmers' choice of words. A lifetime of foolish actions, catching up with him as he'd always somehow envisaged. "Why would I meet with her? What on earth will I say? I'm not going to confess to anything, Ray. Do you think I'm that much of an idiot?"

"No at all, Brad. You are going to tell her that you were one of the first people the police interviewed after the fire because you'd been at the exhibition opening and had bought a drawing, for no other reason than to support the artist. And because Angie had been commissioned by your family to do a portrait. That's all perfectly true. You will tell her that you were shocked and saddened at her death, but that you had nothing to do with it. The police were all over you at the time, there was never anything to find, and you have nothing to hide."

"But what if she has solid evidence?"

"Brad. Stop and think about it. If she had firm evidence, she'd have taken it to the police. She'll be fishing for something to make her case. Your job will be to reassure this woman that the questions about your involvement in this tragic fire have already been asked and answered. She thinks she's about to drop a bombshell on you. You're getting ahead of that wave. You're making it clear to her that broadcasting this story far and wide will get no traction." Chalmers paused, holding Green in his stare. "Let's be clear, Brad, we all want this kept off the airwaves, and this is the first and most important step."

Green was sitting on the edge of his armchair, hunched forward, elbows on knees. "And what is the second step, if she keeps on at me?"

"You leave that to me. If this woman persists despite your explanation, we can make her understand that there are consequences, that no one can spread unfounded rumours without solid proof. Trust me, I have a plan. But you meeting her face to face must come first and you must do your best to reassure her that you were not involved."

Dejected, Green looked up at the retired police chief. He wasn't sure he could pull this off. The thought of initiating engagement with an adversary didn't seem quite right. Still, he knew that he was dependent upon Ray Chalmers, trapped by his past actions, no longer in control of his destiny. "How do I get hold of her?"

"Leave that to me as well Brad. I'll get someone to contact her pretending to be your PA. We'll leave your office team right out of this for now, OK?"

Green nodded, his expression blank.

"Your staff mustn't know anything. Brad. You mustn't tell a soul. Is that clear?"

"Yes. I've got it."

"Once the details are sorted, I'll get back to you. I'll leave it until Monday to establish contact, but I'll aim to set up the meeting for Monday lunchtime. Keep that free until you hear from me."

They shook hands and Green departed. He spent the car trip back to his home rehearsing his lines for his meeting with the podcaster, weighed down by gloomy calculations.

*****

Mark had put up the "closed" sign as soon as Helen and Pat arrived. It was almost five pm in any event, after a steady afternoon in the gallery. They were admiring a beautiful Alison Rehfisch flower study from the nineteen sixties that Mark had just sold to a collector new to his gallery and on behalf of a vendor who was gradually trading more of her works through Beaufort Gallery. It was a radiant piece, yet restrained, and would, Mark thought, enhance any wall on which it was hung.

"So, Galerie Strauss had the details of that exhibition?"

"Sure did," said Helen. "Let me show you."

They all moved behind the computer screen, seated in a semi-circle and leaning in to see the images. Helen uploaded the images from her thumb drive and moved through them quickly, the seven paintings unaccompanied by drawing, the three paired drawings and paintings and, finally, the drawing of the rape scene which they now all inspected.

"Obviously, we all know that there is a painting to accompany this drawing," she said. "We also know that the painting identifies Brad Green—and the artist—much more conspicuously than does the drawing. We know that Brad Green was a keen collector, probably still is, and it is fair to assume that Angie knew Green would visit the exhibition. Which he did, of course, and bought this drawing immediately. According to Judith Strauss, he snatched it off the wall. I think we can all agree he was more than keen that no one else would see it. He'll have destroyed it for sure."

"That suggests that she *did* produce this scene to implicate Brad Green as a rapist," said Mark.

"I think it's possible Angie built the whole theme of violence for this exhibition around her own circumstances so that the image of a rape would seem, at first glance, a logical extension of the series," said Pat. "To most people, it wouldn't have necessarily stood out, especially the drawing which disguises the characters more than the painting. But it would have been plain as day to Brad Green."

"And to his family as well," said Helen. "Angie must've known that he could deny the rape. But identifying him so intimately would have been the ultimate humiliation for him."

"She must have thought better of including the painting in the exhibition, perhaps because it was just too bold," Mark said.

Helen started to speak but paused, as if her thoughts were only now coming into clear alignment. "So, she came up with a drawing that was less obvious on its own but which, in the context of other drawings with related paintings, sent a clear message to Green that there might also be a painting of the rape scene. If she ever decided to display it, it would expose him as her attacker."

"Or maybe just as someone who'd had an affair with her," Mark interjected.

"Either way, the drawing wasn't exposing him so much as provoking him with the threat of exposure should the painting ever be made public."

Pat spoke up. "I think she must have done all of the paintings first but just couldn't bring herself to include this one in the exhibition. I'm not sure if she'd already settled on a theme for the exhibition before she decided she wanted to expose Green, but I reckon she'll have done the four drawings later so that she could use the rape scene drawing, rather than the painting, to get at Green." He smiled. "I think the paintings were the studies for the drawings rather than the reverse. It's almost as if the whole construct of this exhibition, every single work, formed part of plot to threaten Green with public exposure by means of the one painting that, in the end, she didn't even include."

"She must have realised that Green might react badly to the drawing, so she gave the painting to Lisa for safe keeping. That way she could confidently deny it existed," Helen added.

"That abdominal scar is the common clue," said Mark. "Green would have known in a flash that he'd been identified. What does Judith know about all this?"

"I couldn't string her along anymore, Mark. She's an old friend. I sent her an image of the rape scene painting, and she got back to me straight away. She confirmed that the victim is Angie and said that the masked assailant strongly resembles Brad Green as she remembered him, especially the crop of curly hair."

"Does she understand that this is highly confidential, that there are circumstances around this that might even put her at risk? We won't be the only ones who make the link between this crime and her gallery."

"OK. I'll tell her to take copies and wipe her computer. She definitely appreciates that this is serious. I don't know what else I could have told her."

"I get it," said Mark. "And we don't know for sure that there's going to be any trouble. I'd better share this with Aresh, though. And with Lisa and Greta as well. It will certainly strengthen the case for the podcast."

The three gallerists sat in silence for a minute, then headed off to get on with their respective tasks.

Chapter 25
Monday, 12 June 2023

It was after ten am when Lisa headed from Bondi straight into her office in Kellett Street in Potts Point. Greta had set off for work almost two hours earlier; they'd had a great weekend exploring the shops, cafes and walks of the oceanside suburb. She could sense Greta's concerns for their safety, but she was heading back to work this morning feeling positive. Her phone signalled the arrival of a message which she had no choice but to ignore until she settled into a parking spot behind her office block. She didn't recognise the number.

"Hoping to set up a meeting with Brad Green for today. Lunch at the Black Toast Café on Booth Street, Annandale at 1215. Mr Green will be there and he hopes you can join him. Josh Blaire (EA)."

The invitation was clear; Lisa googled the café and wondered about the choice. But the combination of her anonymous note to Brad Green and the announcement of an upcoming podcast had obviously aroused Green's interest and a prompt response, exactly as she'd hoped. She knew she couldn't resist his invitation. *"I will join Mr Green at 1215,"* she replied.

Inside the office, Lisa was greeted with a barrage of messages from her small team. It took her half an hour to clear the backlog and resolve the more urgent decisions, none of which seemed to her to be all that pressing. It was just past eleven am when Lisa got to planning her trip to Annandale. As much as she would like to familiarise herself with the scene, she decided she'd better aim to arrive spot on twelve fifteen, as invited, since Green was possibly meeting other people before and after her. Even still, she'd Uber to within one hundred metres of the café and walk the rest.

Lisa sent Greta an SMS: *"Guess who I'm meeting for lunch?"*

"In a meeting. Can call after midday. Who?"
"Brad Green. Lunch in Annandale."
"What does he want?"
"What do you think? I'm not surprised."
"Forward me his message. Need to be careful."
"At a café on Booth Street. Very public. Sending it now."

*****

Greta forced herself to focus on her work. Green initiating a meeting was unexpected. Something about the arrangement didn't feel right to her. She needed to make some calls but was trapped by work for the moment. She googled Green Enterprises as she feigned concentration on the meeting she was in; she'd ring them as soon as she was free.

*****

Brad Green received a message from an unfamiliar number, seconds after Lisa had responded to her message. *"All set for today. She'll meet you at Black Toast Café on Booth Street. You know the place. Have reserved a table for you outside for 1200. Get there on time and she'll join you around 1215. Don't sit inside in case she's placed someone there to record the conversation. Just reassure her that you've nothing to hide and that the police already know everything there is to know. You'll be great."*

Brad let out a sigh, full of uncertainty.

*****

The other set of messages taking place at this time was between members of the Assassins. First from the boss, Danny, to Carlos: *"Set up on table 2 at 1145. Confirm arrivals and prepare to leave around 1215. Will indicate exact time closer to ETA."*

Carlos: *"Got it Nails"*

Then to Earl: *"Bring vehicle to 1 Gordon at 1130. Await further instructions."*

Earl: *"K"*

*****

Lisa approached the café a little ahead of time. She crossed Booth Street to take in the scene and identified the café which had just two tables of four outside, one closer to the café window, the other alongside it closer to the footpath. There were tables inside but how many was difficult to tell. Each table outside was occupied by a solitary man. Close to the window a sandy-haired man was reading the newspaper and drinking a coffee. Roadside, the man was taller, with curly hair and she knew at a glance it was Brad Green waiting for her to arrive. Her throat tightened. She wished Greta was with her.

Lisa crossed back over Booth Street and walked to the first table. She caught Brad Green's eye and headed towards him. She introduced herself but opted not to seek a handshake. "I'm Lisa Dimopoulos. I'm interested to meet you." She felt awkward but she could detect no malice in Green's eyes, and she felt surprisingly at ease, as if it was him who was more nervous than her.

"Thanks for meeting me at such short notice. Please, sit down. Can I get you a coffee? Would you like some lunch?"

"I'll have a long mac," said Lisa.

At the next table, Carlos sent a message: *"Both in position. Coffees being ordered."*

From Nails: *"ETA 5 minutes. Leave in 4."*

Lisa's phone rang; she could see it was Greta calling. She tapped the automatic reply *"Can I call you later?"*

She looked up at Brad Green and set the phone down on the table. "I'm wondering what prompted you to arrange this meeting?" she asked.

Having bided his time, Carlos stood up and left his table, walking out on to Booth Street, heading west.

Lisa's phone binged. It was from Greta: *"Need to talk, urgent."*

"I'm sorry, I'd better reply," she said before Green could say anything. She tapped out her reply: *"Just sat down, seems OK to me."*

Greta: *"Are you inside or outside?"*

Lisa looked up at Brad Green, a little flustered. "It's my partner, harassing me, I'm so sorry," she said.

"No worries, you take your time," said Green.

Lisa turned away and typed back: *"Outside by the road."*

Greta: *"Get inside NOW Please call me NOW"*

Angry bells rang inside Lisa's head. She hated being bossed around. This was not like Greta, or at least she hadn't seen this side of her so far. She excused herself from the table and went inside as she called her girlfriend. "What's up Greta, you sound mighty agitated?"

"Are you inside yet?"

"Yes, I am inside," her annoyance transparent, "and Brad Green seems perfectly sane."

"Please listen to me carefully. Get to the very back of the café now. Do what I'm asking you."

"Yes, yes, for fuck's sake, Greta, I'm almost out of the back bloody door. Is that enough for you?"

"I rang Green Enterprises and there's no one there by the name of Josh or Joshua or Blaire or anyone at all. Brad Green's EA's name is Maddy. This is a setup. I think you and Brad Green are both being targeted. Do not go back outside."

Lisa was speechless. It sounded fanciful, almost demented. Before she could say anything, the outside of the café erupted in a deafening explosion of noise, like a massive detonation of firecrackers, accompanied by the shattering of glass. Lisa dropped to the ground—stunned, not hurt—the sound of a motorcycle speeding down Booth Street leading into a short silence and then screams of distress.

"Are you there Lisa? Are you still there?"

"I think they've blown him up."

"Are you hurt?"

"No. What do I do?"

"Just walk out. As calmly as you can. Walk out and turn right up Booth Street. I promise you, they won't be coming back, so just keep walking steadily and keep talking to me, OK?"

Lisa stood up, surrounded by frightened faces and people on phones, frozen to their seats. Glass had blasted in every direction, a few tiny shards even reaching her at the back of the café. She put the phone to her ear, as if to harness some of Greta's confidence and control and headed for the front door. Outside she turned right and walked, dazed and confused east on Booth Street. She refused to look in the direction of her table but the glimpse she caught of blood on the pavement was enough to turn her stomach.

"I'm out. There's blood everywhere."

"Don't look back, sweetheart. You've done incredibly well. Just keep walking. The first right is Trafalgar Street, turn right up Trafalgar and keep walking. Are you following me?" Greta had Google Maps of the area opened on her work laptop.

"I'm on Trafalgar. Where am I going?"

"A bit further, on your left is a small park, at Piper Street South. There's a bench there. I want you to find that bench and just sit down. You keep talking to me."

Sirens howled in the background, ambulance and police hurtling towards the café. Lisa walked forward, oblivious to the beautiful homes lining the street, reliant upon Greta's guiding voice. The small park approached her on the left and she felt herself cross the road, looking for a bench to sit on as instructed. Close to some playground equipment, she found the bench and sat down. "I'm here."

"You're safe now Lisa. I'm coming to collect you. I'll be about twenty minutes. Can you stay put for that long? I'll call you again as soon as I'm in my car."

"I won't be moving anywhere until you get here. I think he's been killed. I think I was also supposed to be killed. I think we were both meant to die."

"I am sorry, Lisa. I didn't see this coming. I put you at risk."

"You saved my life, Greta." Lisa was shaking now. "Just come and get me, please. I'm scared."

*****

Earl had decided to take out Brad Green knowing that the female party was unexpectedly not in sight. He'd called in as his driver sped away from the scene. "She wasn't at the table, Nails. I made the call and took out Green. He won't survive. No major collateral damage. We're just heading on to Pyrmont Bridge now, ETA ninety seconds. Get the door up and we'll drive right up into the truck."

"Good call, Earl," said Finnerty wondering about the improbable absence of the podcaster. "Green was the main target. I'll let the copper know. Get back quick."

The motorbike slowed down as they drove up Gordon Street turning into the storeroom through the first wide door and up the gangplank onto the truck. They killed the bike's engine, secured it with straps, removed the gangplank and shut the truck's back door. The truck headed off immediately, turning one hundred and eighty degrees in the large interior space and emerging out of the second garage door alongside. Carlos was at the wheel of the truck; Earl joined him in the passenger seat, and they set off towards the west, heading for Chalmers' Mulgoa property.

"Ray." Finnerty was now on the phone to Chalmers.

"Yes, Danny."

"We got Green, but the girl disappeared at the last minute. No idea if she went missing by chance or if she was warned. But we made the call to take out Green."

"That's … interesting. And disappointing. But I agree with the decision. Is the bike on its way here?"

"Yes, Carlos and Earl are on their way."

"I'll transfer the agreed sum tonight. I'd like you to execute the next phase this evening if you're able to. There is no time to watch and wait."

"Will do."

*****

Lisa was sitting upright on a bench at the western end of Hinsby Park. Greta pulled up alongside the park and exited the car, walking straight to Lisa. She sat next to her and held her hand, the fine flecks of glass embedded in Lisa's black jacket sparkling in the sunlight. "How are you feeling?"

"Overwhelmed." She slowly shook her head. "These people never get caught, do they? They just kill people and get away with it. Maybe they'll try and get me again? I don't have a chance. I think I'm screwed."

"Let's just get you home to my place. You'll be safe there. Will you let me secure your office? I think it's at risk right now and you don't want any important information or material being damaged."

Lisa looked at Greta, a hollow expression on her face. "And my home too? Will I even be safe there?"

"Lisa, darling. Not right now. You're not safe. But I'll look after you and we will find out who is behind all this. Whoever Brad Green approached for help all those years ago must have bikie connections. And anyone else who knew about that help is in peril. I'll make some calls, but you're coming back to my place right now and I'll head off to Pott's Point as soon as you're settled."

*****

News of the gangland-style killing was all over the radio as they battled their way through traffic to Bondi. There was little of substance to the reporting, and no mention of Brad Green who was an unlikely underworld figure and not on anyone's radar as such. Once identified, his family would be swarmed by the police and the media. It would be good to get ahead of them, thought Greta. She would ask Lisa's team to track Green's parents down.

As she drove, she wondered if she should call Gary Frobisher. Was he the person with the connection to the underworld? She realised that she needed an ally with influence and intelligence inside the force. Maybe she'd try Luke Brand again. That, she knew, would have to wait until Lisa was safe in Bondi.

*****

It was mid-afternoon before Greta left her home. She'd undressed Lisa and insisted she take a shower; then had put her in a dressing gown and sent her to bed where she'd collapsed and fallen asleep.

In her car, Greta called Lisa's office and explained what had happened. The news that their boss had been within metres of the gangland murder was a shock. Nevertheless, they accepted Greta's instructions and immediately packed up their computers and all the paperwork they had. Greta joined them to help and asked if someone could help locate the Green family residence and contact details. By six pm the office was stripped bare. They agreed to bring the materials to Bondi although Greta didn't yet know where she would put it all.

A small convoy of cars made its way back to her Bondi semi-detached. Greta had called Susan Lieb and asked if she had enough room in their garage to store some computers and other things related to her work. Without hesitation, Susan had agreed, provided she could come over with some food and meet Greta's new friend. With the Liebs, it was always a balance between genuine neighbourliness and outright intrusion; on this occasion, Greta had no choice but to accept the intrusion. At least the food would be great, that much she knew.

The podcast team unloaded the materials into the Lieb's garage. Then they all filed into Greta's flat, the team to check on their boss, Susan Lieb to check her out. They stayed for a quick feed and a cup of tea and it was after eight pm when Greta ushered them out of her home. She stepped out of her front door, closed it behind her and rang the home number she had been given for Elizabeth and Sam Green.

"Hello?"

Greta heard the voice of an older woman and could detect doubt, almost fear in her tentative greeting. "Is this Elizabeth Green?"

"Yes. Who is this? Is this the police? Is this about Bradley?"

Greta imagined that, at the very least, Elizabeth Green must have been worried that her son was missing although he had not yet been publicly identified. "I *do* work for the police, Mrs Green. And this *is* about Bradley. Am I the first person from the police that has been in touch?"

"Yes. What has happened to him. None of us has heard from him and there was that awful incident in Annandale. I can assure you he's had no dealings with underworld figures. He's never been into drugs. He might be a lazy so-and-so, but he hasn't been mixed up with bikies; and he is my boy."

From her time in the Major Crime Squad, Greta remembered the pain of breaking bad news. Although it had been the worst part of the job, it had by a long way been the most important part to get right. "I am afraid that your Brad was the target of that attack. And I am afraid it was something to do with people he had dealt with back in 2010. Do you remember there was a house fire in which a young woman died and with whom your son was involved?"

Greta heard Elizabeth Green exhale slowly. She continued. "I think that the truth of those events has only just emerged and the people who helped Brad back then wanted him to be silenced. It's an awful situation, but I'm afraid your son has been murdered by people he once trusted."

Elizabeth's voice was quiet and unsteady. "When he didn't answer the phone—for me or his office staff—I knew he was in trouble." There was a long pause. "How can I trust you any more than we could that bastard? My Sam had to sell himself to that devil, to get Bradley out of trouble. He built himself a mansion in the national park with the proceeds. Robbed us of a family treasure. We've never been free of him. But who are you? Are you even with the police?"

"I am with the police but, I'm so sorry, I cannot tell you my name. I think they're after me as well. Elizabeth, I suspect the Major Crime team will soon be in touch with you and they will want to know all about the trouble Brad got into and all about the people who helped him get out of it. Meanwhile, I think you might also be at some risk. Anyone who knows about that house fire could be targeted the same way Bradley was. These people are ruthless."

"What would they want with me? I'm hardly going to betray my own people. My husband is still alive. I have a family to consider, to take care of."

"I doubt whoever is behind this would take your word on that. They know you'll figure out that it was them. And that you might be angry enough to dob them in. Would you be prepared to tell me who you dealt with back in 2010? Was it Gary Frobisher?"

"No. He was just one of the investigating officers. The man we had to deal with was Raymond Chalmers. You get him for me. He is pure evil." And the call ended before Greta could repeat her warning.

Retired Assistant Commissioner Ray Chalmers. That's who was behind this. Backed up by a slick and violent bikie gang. Greta realised they were all in harm's way; she called Luke Brand.

"Brand, here. What nonsense have you got for me this time, McCartney? I'm sure you know we're reasonably busy right now."

Greta had no time for Luke's haughty tone. "Do you know where Elizabeth Green is, Luke?"

There was no reply, Greta imagining Luke's surprise that she might know that the roadside killing had involved a member of the Green family.

"She'll be as dead as her son by morning if you don't get to her straight away. Unless he's got to her already. You know who's behind this, or you should do."

"I have no idea how you know about Brad Green, but you'd better have a bloody good explanation. We were planning to see Mrs Green first thing tomorrow. Her son was nothing more than a spoiled brat-freeloader who probably owed a gang some money. His mum'll have nothing to do with this."

"Oh yes, she does. She knows exactly why her son was targeted and that puts her right in the firing line. Brad Green was involved in the murder of a young female artist in a house fire back in 2010 and Ray Chalmers took money from the family to fix the investigation. Now he's orchestrating this mayhem to cover his tracks and he will wipe out anyone he even dreams might be able to expose him."

"Oh, come off it, Greta. Ray Chalmers? That's bullshit. You're just making this up as you go. You've never recovered from being dumped from Major Crime."

The sneer in Luke' voice was unmistakeable, but Greta detected a kernel of self-doubt quivering beneath his strident tone. She closed her eyes and caught her breath. "Elizabeth Green knows precisely what price Chalmers extracted from her family to close down the investigation into the fire, to make sure her son's involvement was hidden. He'll want to know who else she might have told, and he'll be sure to have her and anyone else who knows silenced."

"Greta, this is delusional. Chalmers was crooked, for sure, but no more than plenty of others. How do you know it was him? Why am I only hearing this now?"

"Elizabeth Green told me maybe five minutes ago. Chalmers' men will be there tonight, Luke. You'll be too late by morning."

"Ahhh! Fuck you, McCartney. You're full of shit. You've become a total pain in the arse. You're just wasting my time. Just … fuck off."

The phone went silent. To Greta, that felt like the end of their fragile friendship. But she hoped that a life might have been saved. She rang Mark Lewis.

"Hi Greta. It's a little late for you, isn't it?"

"It's been a big day here, Mark, and things have turned angry. You heard about the gangland killing in Sydney?"

"Yes, it's just been on the news. Bikie retribution, they're saying."

"I'm afraid not. It was Brad Green who was murdered, and Lisa was literally metres away. She was also a target. She escaped by chance alone."

"Shit. That's … scary."

"The situation here has deteriorated, Mark, and I need to warn you that some of these bikie gangs have national reach and that you mustn't share any of our information with anyone at all. Whoever knows about this—Linda, Helen, Pat, Aresh—they're all at risk. The people who killed Brad Green will do anything to protect their interests. We've got to get to them first."

"As far as I know, it's just us for now. The painting is in my gallery. I don't think they'd have any reason to link it to Perth."

"OK, that's good. Please keep it close to your chest. And tell the others the same. Lisa was very nearly murdered today."

"Is she OK?"

"Shaken, for sure, but she's not injured."

"I was going to call you anyway, Greta. We got some more information about the original exhibition. Helen tracked down the images from the gallery and there was a drawing—just a small piece in ink and pen—of the rape scene in that exhibition. The gallerist remembered that it was Brad Green who had bought it. Green will have recognised the scene and suspected there was a painting to accompany it. He probably went to Angie's home to find it and to get her to give it to him … but if he's been killed, I'm not sure how much difference this all makes anymore."

"Who provided Helen with those images? Is she here in Sydney?"

"Judith Strauss. She was a gallerist in Woollahra, and she represented Angie Richards at the time of the exhibition. Her gallery closed years ago, but she and Helen are still on good terms. Judith sent the images of that exhibition through to her."

"Do you know how much Helen told her?"

"Helen said she sent Judith a copy of Angie's painting. Judith recognised Brad Green straight away. It was definitely him in the painting. But we told Judith to delete the image she'd been sent. If they do track her down, there'll be nothing to prove any connection she has to that painting or to Perth."

"I don't think you really know how these people work, Mark. Do you have Helen's number? Please, I need to warn Judith immediately."

"Of course," and Mark messaged Helen's phone number as she spoke. "And I'll send you Pat's as well. In case." Within seconds, Greta had both numbers. She finished her call with Mark and rang Helen, but the line was engaged. She hung up rather than wait for the voicemail message and called Pat.

"Hello?"

"Pat, this is Greta McCartney, from Sydney."

"Sure, Greta. Mark is on the phone to Helen right this minute. I hope we haven't done the wrong thing."

"It's probably too soon to tell, but I need to contact Judith Strauss urgently. Does Helen have her phone number?"

"She does, and we can send it through straight away."

"Thanks. And do you know where she lives?"

"Let me check. Helen's free now."

Seconds passed slowly. "Hi Greta." It was Helen. "I've got her address here on her email. It's Five Pickering Lane, Woollahra. Not far from where her old gallery was. I'll text you the phone number too."

"Thanks Helen. I'm going there now. If there's been any trouble, they might have found enough to link it back to you. The sort of people who murdered Brad Green today will do whatever it takes to protect their interests. You and Pat should get ready to leave home tonight, just in case. Wait for me to tell you but, if you do have to leave, take your computers and phones and anything else at all that indicates who you might have shared this information with. They'll keep going until they destroy everything they think needs to be destroyed."

As soon as she'd completed the call to Helen, Greta stepped back inside, grabbed her keys, dashed across to the sofa and kissed Lisa goodnight before she headed out to her car. Her phone binged, announcing the arrival of Judith Strauss's contact details. Greta placed her 0.40 Glock beneath the driver's seat and rang Judith's number before starting the engine. There was no answer. A bead of dread formed in her mind.

Then she messaged Luke Brand. "*I have grave concerns about the gallerist who handled that artist's works in 2010. Judith Strauss – 5 Pickering Lane, Woollahra. I'm going there now. You do what you think's right.*" She didn't expect a response; she started her car and sped off to the Woollahra address.

Within a minute, her car phone rang. It was Luke. "Greta? Something's up at the Green household. It's all turning to shit. And, thanks, I've just sent a car to Pickering Lane. If you're going, go armed."

"Sure. On my way. Let me know what's happened at the Greens."

He hung up.

Greta got onto Old South Head Road, headed south and west onto Edgecliff Road and veered left onto Queen Street. A right turn and then a left and, in a matter of seconds, she was on Pickering Lane. The narrow street was silent.

Heading west, the street numbers were confusing. On her left were the rear garages of houses evidently fronting on to a street running parallel. Midway, on her right, she saw number five, a double-storey weatherboard house with a shallow porch and a few steps leading up to the front door. No lights were on inside.

She picked up her pistol and tried to collect her thoughts, pondering the wisdom of entering the house on her own. Car lights appeared at the western end of the lane, the flashing lights on the roof indicating that it was Luke's team. She exited her car and signalled to them; the police car sped up and parked just outside number five. Between the two parked vehicles, facing in opposite directions, there was now no way any other vehicle could get through the narrow road.

"Greta McCartney," she said, showing her badge, "I'm with Fraud."

"Yep, Luke's told us to expect you. Have you seen anything?" Both policemen were young, in their twenties, Greta estimated. It was the older of the two who had spoken.

"I just got here. Shall we go in?"

They walked to the front door and went to knock. The door was ajar and swung open with minimal pressure. They drew their weapons, and the older policeman signalled his partner to cover him as he entered; Greta followed. She found the light switch and tried to turn it on, but the power had been disconnected. She withdrew her torch to illuminate the path for her colleagues. The silence in the house was suffocating and Greta could detect the odour of blood thick in the air. She knew they were too late.

They walked through the lounge room, a half-filled cup of tea sitting on a small table alongside an empty lounge chair facing a blank television screen. Through a glass door, sprawled on the floor, was a woman, perhaps in her seventies, with an obvious head wound and blood and human tissue sprayed across the carpet and wall to her left. The room that had the appearance of a study. One wall was occupied by a full-length bookcase packed with books almost all of which Greta could see, at a glance, were about art. The spine of "Brett Whiteley. Art and Life" caught her eye.

There was a desk with a computer screen, mouse and keyboard still present but no obvious laptop or hard drive. Various cables had been pulled out and left exposed, like plumbing pipes on a construction site. The three police completed the search of the house including the second floor. The assailants had been and gone; and they appeared to have taken what they'd come for. The policeman called his boss: "Hi Luke. We have a body here, probably Judith Strauss, no sign of life. Looks like they got what they needed, took the laptop and left. I'll call forensics and the ambulance."

When he finished the call, Greta spoke up: "They won't take long to figure out that there's a connection to people in Perth. There's evidence of the original crime over there too. I need to get them some protection."

The policemen looked at her warily. "You'd better discuss that with Luke."

"Sure," Greta replied, knowing that she had a number of calls she had to make without delay.

First, she messaged Luke Brand: "*Judith Strauss murdered. Did they get Elizabeth Green? We need to let Perth know. Lots of people at risk.*"

And she called Helen O'Beirne: "Hi Helen, its Greta. Are you and Pat ready to get out? I mean right away?"

"Is Judith OK?"

"Right now, I just can't vouch for her safety, so I've got to get you and Pat out of sight. Can you leave this instant?"

"Yes. We're ready to leave."

"And you've removed all traces of the painting and all electronic devices that might have a record of it as well?"

"Yes, but there's probably stuff in our warehouse and in the gallery as well."

Greta felt overwhelmed. Chalmers could access this information at any number of places and there was no way she could plug all the holes. "Don't worry about the warehouse or the gallery. It's you two who most need to hide. Just get to a city hotel straight away and spend the night there. I'll keep you posted."

Next, she rang Mark Lewis. "Mark, it's Greta. I think you or your gallery might be targeted sometime soon. Can you and Linda get to a safe place, a hotel maybe, tonight? There've been more attacks here this evening and you need to protect yourselves first and foremost."

"Bloody hell. Who else has been targeted? Not Judith?"

"I can't say, Mark, but these people are serious criminals. Get the painting. And both of you have to get to a safe place. You need to move now."

"I went in and got Angie's painting straight away, after your call. I'll take it with us now. Are the others OK?"

"Helen and Pat are probably the next ones they'll go for. They're already on their way to a hotel. I'll call Aresh now. I don't think they'll make that connection too quickly, but you never know."

Mark assured her he and Linda would leave without delay. Finally, she rang Aresh.

"Hi, this is Dr Aresh Mehta. I'm sorry I couldn't get to your call …"

Greta groaned at the recorded message, waited until it had finished and left a voice mail. "Aresh. Greta McCartney in Sydney here. Please call me without delay, as soon as you get this message. I'll send an SMS as well."

The SMS: "*Aresh. Urgent issues have arisen. Please call immediately. Greta McCartney*"

Her phone rang that instant. It was Luke Brand.

"Hi, Luke. This is awful."

"Yep. I'm at the Green household. Elizabeth Green's been shot and killed. Same as in Woollahra from what I'm told. Listen, that podcaster's in serious trouble. Do you know where she is?"

"No idea. No idea where she lives but her office is in Pott's Point. Should we check it out?"

"CCTV shows she was at the café this afternoon, meeting with Brad Green. She left immediately after the attack, just walked away. We don't know where she went. I'm not sure if she was a target or if she was part of the setup. She might have lured him into the trap."

"Don't know, Luke," she lied. "But Elizabeth Green told me that Ray Chalmers was the man who they paid off to protect her son. And it'll be him and not that podcaster pulling these strings. No way she could orchestrate this sort of mayhem. We need to get to him, not her."

"I've called her number but it's not answering. She might also be dead. I've sent a car to their office, so no need for you to go there as well. Could be bad."

"Where does Chalmers live?"

"His home is in Balmain. We've been there already but the place is deserted. And he's not answering his phone either. All we've got to go on him is what you say Elizabeth Green told you. I have a feeling that this is going to burn itself out soon enough and we'll have nothing to pin on anyone. And we've got three bodies already."

Greta's phone indicated an incoming call from Aresh. She ended her call with Luke Brand and answered Aresh. "Hi Aresh, Greta here."

"What's the urgency, Greta? You're sounding a bit panicky."

"So far, three people have been murdered today in Sydney in respect of that painting of yours. Take it from me, Aresh, there are good grounds for panic."

Aresh fell silent, a little scolded, Greta could sense. Good, she thought, this was no time to downplay the gravity of the situation.

"It's not your fault, Aresh. But the people who helped Brad Green get out of trouble back in 2010 are doing everything they possibly can to silence anyone they think knows what happened. Bikies got to Brad Green this morning, they've killed his mother and now they've killed the person whose gallery exhibited

Angie's works back in 2010. They're all dead and they nearly got Lisa this morning at the café. If they haven't already figured out that there's a painting at the heart of this and that the painting is in Perth, they soon will."

Aresh went quiet. "They killed his mother? But the painting implicates Brad Green as a rapist. It doesn't point to any murder, and it doesn't identify anyone who helped him cover it up. Surely whoever did help him will soon realise that the painting isn't their problem after all. Other than the people who covered this up in the first place, who else could implicate them."

Probably only me, thought Greta. "I'm fairly certain Elizabeth Green knew about the deal that protected her son, which is why she's been killed. But you may be right, Aresh. Maybe no-one else knows who helped the Greens or who is behind today's chaos." Greta paused, choosing her words carefully. "But the painting contains evidence from the crime scene, that cigarette lighter for sure, and today's events are going to mean that the whole Surry Hills fire investigation will need to be re-opened. Every bit of evidence that points to the bigger crime will need to be controlled by the perpetrators if they are to get out of this. They are ruthless and we're all in danger, even you in Perth."

"You too, Greta. And Lisa. Jesus. They tried to kill her?"

"No doubt about that. But the best way for you to help us is to get to a safe place right away and to keep your head down until I call you back."

"Shouldn't we involve the police here as well? I mean, surely we should be protected by professionals?"

"New South Wales police have already alerted their counterparts in Perth. That part of the investigation is now in the hands of organised crime specialists. But they cannot cover multiple homes and offices as quickly as or as effectively as you might imagine. You need to look out for yourself."

Aresh had moved out onto the footpath, having to escape the racket inside the bar to take the call. He and Cathy had been out for a drink, celebrating the completion of her exams and re-calibrating their feelings and their prospects together. "What about the painting?"

"Mark's got it and he's taking it with him into hiding. I don't know what these criminals are going to do next, if anything. But they are hunting down the people who they think can provide them with important information and, when they find them, they've been killing them. Honestly, Aresh, this is no time to hope for the best. Just hide tonight and we can regroup tomorrow. Tell me as soon as you're settled in a hotel. Look, I have to go now, but please promise me you will get out of your home now."

"Did they kill Mrs Green *at* her home?"

"Yes, why do you ask?"

"I just wondered if you'd been there. To their study. The scene of the painting."

"I haven't. Does it still matter?"

"I suppose not. It's just that …. no. It doesn't really matter."

Greta thought for a moment. "You're right. That could validate the painting. That's not a bad idea. I should check it out. I'll let you know if I'm allowed in."

Aresh assured Greta he would stay safe and ended their exchange. He wasn't sure he fancied hiding in a hotel room.

*****

"What was that?" Cathy had been drawn out of the bar towards the phone conversation. Besk was packed, more than usual for a weeknight, and it was something in the way Aresh had exited the building, as he listened to his voicemail, that had made Cathy abandon their table to follow him.

"Greta says that it was Brad Green who was murdered this morning at that café shooting that was on the news tonight. They were probably targeting Lisa as well and nearly killed her. And now they've killed Green's mother." Aresh exhaled, his expression a mixture of confusion and worry. "It doesn't really make sense. She says I have to get out of my home tonight in case they try to get to me. But, if they can figure out that I'm involved, they might figure out that you are too. Maybe you should hide too."

"OK. Let's move." Cathy grasped Aresh's arm and pulled him forwards, down Railway Road towards his car. "We'd better not fool with these people. We can grab some gear and even stay at a hotel."

"Hang on," Aresh said, holding his ground. "Let me think this through. I don't want to hide in a hotel. Surely they're not going to be chasing people down in Perth over a painting?"

Cathy stared at Aresh, trying hard to understand him but, in an instant, aware of a growing distance between them. "From what you say, Greta was pretty clear. You might be in danger. You can't just go home and hope for the best."

"I don't know. I think this is all crazy. I'm not into this cops-and-robbers' nonsense. We were supposed to be toasting you and … talking about us."

"I get that, Aresh. We could talk at the hotel." Cathy searched Aresh's eyes for a flicker of comprehension, a trace of connection. Aresh remained silent. "Alright. You do what you think you need to. I'm going to head home and grab some things and spend the night at my parents' place." She waited again for him to respond, but his expression remained blank.

"Goodnight Aresh." Cathy turned, walked away and summoned an Uber while Aresh watched on, rooted to the spot.

*****

"What've you got, Danny."

"I've just sent you an image of a painting we found on the Woollahra laptop. We found the email in her Trash folder. It appears to have been painted in 2010 and has recently resurfaced. According to the woman in Woollahra, it identifies Brad Green as the rapist. It's undoubtedly what's prompted the current interest. She got the image from a colleague in Perth who has the painting."

"Perth? Shit. Did she know anything about me or the Assassins?"

"Not that she indicated, Ray. I'm sure she was telling the truth."

Chalmers was in no doubt that she had been. "And Elizabeth Green?"

"Carlos went there. The old lady was defiant and mouthing off – I'm sure you made the right call. He said she'd literally just spoken to the police and that she boasted that she'd named you. I've no idea who she spoke to. She said it was a policewoman who had refused to identify herself. It might have been the podcaster fishing for information. But Carlos thought she was telling the truth on all counts. Either way, you might assume that your cover has been blown."

"And the podcaster's office? Was there anything there?"

"Earl went there and found it cleaned out. Barely a paper scrap. They must have anticipated someone coming. That podcaster is one calculating bitch."

"I don't know. She went to the café this morning and I reckon she was tipped off and only then just in time. I think she's been working with someone inside the force, someone who is helping her anticipate what will happen. I think we can also assume that the person in Perth has been warned already. But I want you to check that out, Danny. You've got a unit in the West. Get them to that person's house as soon as possible. If they've cleared out then we'll know for sure they're getting help from inside the force. We can regroup and plan the next steps. If they haven't, then we find out everything we can and leave no trace."

"This is becoming a big job, Ray."

"Don't worry, Danny, you'll be rewarded."

Chapter 26
Tuesday, 13 June 2023

By midnight Sydney time, Greta was back in Bondi, Lisa having regained her composure even after all of the day's grisly details were recounted. In Perth, Helen and Pat, Linda and Mark were sitting in their respective hotel rooms located at the eastern end of Perth's central business district. They joined the online meeting within seconds of Greta initiating it. Aresh joined from his Leederville study.

"Thanks for joining in. Lisa's here and she's doing much better. I need to tell you some awful news. You know that Elizabeth Green, Brad Green's mother, was murdered in her home this evening. At about the same time, Judith Strauss's home in Woollahra was broken into." Greta paused, knowing that this would give the others time to prepare for what followed. "I went there myself, as soon as Helen sent me their address, but it was already too late. She has also been murdered."

Helen clasped her hands to her mouth muffling a cry.

"It's been a very scary day, all round," said Lisa. "I apologise for embroiling you all in our bikie violence and I am just so sorry for Helen's friend here." Her voice broke and she had to sit back, out of camera shot. Greta put an arm around her. Mark could hear the soothing tone of her words to Lisa. Pat consoled Helen. The Perth crew waited.

Greta turned back to the screen and continued, trying to disguise her rising apprehension. "So, just to reassure you, New South Wales police have their gloves well and truly off. There are a limited number of gangs that can orchestrate this sort of violence. Their names are irrelevant right now, but two of them are national organisations and I'm anxious that one of those two gangs might be involved. The police are endeavouring to shut them all down right now, but the gangs are pretty good at hiding evidence. We've seen the bike they used for this morning's café strike on CCTV, but it hasn't been found anywhere yet. The more important thing for the police at the moment is just to limit the gang's ability to shed any more blood."

"Won't that gang be acting on instructions?" asked Aresh. "I mean, bikies wouldn't really be interested in Brad Green, let alone the others."

"I think you're right. The Major Crime people have told me that they have some information about a senior policeman, possibly retired, who had bikie connections, that might point to him being involved." Greta maintained her impassive expression. "They're looking into that, but they've given me no name so far."

Lisa's phone rang in the background, and she stepped out of the room to take the call.

"The reason I've asked you to get out of your homes is that these people want the information you have more than they want to figure out what's on your laptops. It's not that they wouldn't take all that stuff as well, it's just that they know how … to get to the truth." She paused and Mark imagined that Greta was considering whether or not to explain what she meant in more detail.

Greta continued. "And that will give them a good idea about what their adversaries know. Getting you out of your homes is the best way to keep them away from you altogether."

Aresh remained silent.

"Are you saying that they got information out of Judith Strauss and Elizabeth Green?" asked Mark.

"I'm afraid we need to assume that these people know whatever Judith and Elizabeth knew."

Mark observed Helen and Pat turn to face each other as Lisa re-joined them on the screen. "That was Claire from my podcast team on the phone," she said. "There's been a break-in at my office in Potts Point. But Greta had them clean it out so there was nothing to take. That's twice in one day, Gret. Thanks."

Greta nodded and continued. "A lot depends upon whether the assailants believe that the police already have a clear idea who is behind all this. If they believe that the police are just guessing, they'll likely lay low and see if they can ride out the storm. After all, Brad Green and his mother are both gone, and they were probably the only ones who knew the full story."

This time, Pat's phone rang, startling him and Helen. He grabbed at his phone but dropped it on the hotel floor before stooping to pick it up and walking away from the screen.

"There's a sister too, isn't there? She might be at risk," added Mark.

"How long will it take for us to be able to get back to some sort of normality?" asked Linda not waiting for an answer to Mark's question. "We can't stay here for ever."

"I get it," said Greta. "I've contacted WA Police and they're figuring out what they need to do to help you."

Pat re-joined the conversation. "That was our police. There's been a break-in at our home – you were right Greta." Helen gasped, anger rising in her expression. "Seems as if the police here already know who we are and why there's been a break-in. Not a lot of damage, luckily. They took an old PC but we've got the current ones here with us." Mark thought Pat sounded remarkably calm and noted his cool expression.

"That's clear then," said Greta. "They must have found out about Helen and Pat from Judith." She paused. "So, they'll also know about the painting. They've probably also seen it on Judith's laptop. Aresh suggested I go to the Green's home to see if the study in Angie's painting is theirs. I'll try to get to there this evening, although it's probably no longer the most vital piece of evidence."

"Can I say something?" It was Aresh, who had blurred the backdrop to his screen image. They all waited, Cathy's absence and the suspicion that he had dialled in from home hanging uncomfortably in the air. "These criminals must have been surprised, let's say, that Lisa was able to avoid being shot this morning. And that Lisa's team had cleared out their office in quick time. And that Helen and Pat weren't at home, just now, when they'd have been expected to be there."

The group were silent, waiting for him to get to the point. "They've probably figured out that someone's helping us, Greta. I reckon you two are more at risk than the rest of us put together. And especially if you say there's a retired policeman involved in all this."

"They obviously know about Lisa," Greta said. "And I've put steps in place to protect her. So far, the only people who know for sure that I am involved are people I think we can trust."

There was silence, then a brief discussion to arrange a time for the next update, and they signed off.

*****

Despite the late hour, Ray Chalmers was wide awake. He had just called Danny Finnerty to direct him to stand down the team in Perth. He felt that he now had a better grasp of the situation he faced. The painting of Brad Green supposedly raping that artist was in Perth and he suspected that it had been brought to Helen O'Beirne in the course of her job. She must have tracked down the original gallery in Sydney and had then shared it with Judith Strauss. Strauss had identified Green as the assailant, given that he was a former customer. It still wasn't clear to him how all this had subsequently made it to Lisa Dimopoulos; according to Earl, the Woollahra gallerist had not known anything about her.

His thoughts were swirling. He couldn't imagine who inside the force would've been interested in re-opening the case; he was confident people loyal to him would have actively discouraged any new investigation. By whichever means the podcaster had come to suspect a cover-up in the original fire investigation, she could not possibly have predicted the events of the previous twelve hours.

The podcaster, her office team and the O'Beirne woman in Perth had all been sent into hiding. Without doubt, someone who understood how things might play out was pulling these strings. He was certain that this was the woman who had rung Elizabeth Green just before Carlos had got to her. It made sense to him that the woman who made that call was a police officer, familiar with the world of major crime, perhaps disgruntled that her colleagues were refusing to re-investigate what she thought was a significant new lead in the fire investigation. And, now, aware that he was at the heart of it all. The only solid evidence that pointed to Chalmers' involvement, as far as he knew, was Elizabeth Green's testimony over the phone, given to a woman who had claimed to be police.

The painting was in Perth, of all places. How had the connection between it and the fire been made? How had the podcaster come to be involved? And what was driving this policewoman to help them all? What else might she know about him?

He hadn't figured it all out by a long way, but he knew that she remained his primary target. He didn't care how long the others stayed out of the picture; this treacherous policewoman had to be dealt with.

Frobisher remained uncontactable, of no help to him at all. Still, there were others inside the force who might have an idea who this woman was – he would double-down on Paul Lenzo first thing in the morning.

*****

Greta phoned Luke Brand as soon as the group call ended. "Have you heard there was a break-in in Perth?"

"Yes, we're all over it. No one was home. That was the right advice, Greta, well done. There's been a huge response here. There've been raids on multiple gang headquarters. Lots of weapons have been seized and some vehicles have been confiscated. All the gangs are laying low for now, so I'm not expecting any more fireworks in the next day or two, at least not here in Sydney. But I reckon they knew this is how we would react, and I'd be surprised if we find anything that links any of them to the killings. We're trying to piece together CCTV from Annandale but so far we've got nothing of any use."

"Ray Chalmers will be behind this …"

"That's not going to be easy to …"

"I don't have time for niceties here, Luke. What we can prove is one thing, I know that. But what we believe is quite another, and I absolutely know that Elizabeth Green was telling the truth about Chalmers. And that he now knows that someone who said that she was a policewoman has been given his name. I don't know what's happening with Gary. Maybe he's also been taken out or maybe he's gone to ground. Maybe he told Chalmers about me before he disappeared, maybe he didn't."

"Yeah. I can't get hold of him at all. I reckon he'll have gone into hiding. He was mates with Chalmers, but Gary always played his cards very close to his chest. The way you've explained it to me, Brad Green will have gone straight to Chalmers when he received that anonymous threat. And Chalmers would then have gone straight to Frobisher. No one here other than me is owning up to talking to either Frobisher—or Chalmers for that matter—in the last fortnight, but Chalmers still has people loyal to him in all parts of the force."

"I inquired inside the Arson Squad about ten days ago and everyone there will now know that it was me who made that call. Chalmers will find a way to find out. And I think Chalmers might still try and track the podcaster down as well. My feeling is that we need to get to him before he gets to us."

Greta was aware of Lisa sitting beside her, listening to the conversation, her fear about the relentless intent of these criminals palpable. Brand's silence seemed only to confirm those thoughts. Before he could answer, Greta asked: "Do you think you can get me into the Green's house? I'm keen to see if there's a room in the house that lines up with the painting they've got in Perth."

"I don't see why not. I'm still here. Come on over and we can make a night of it."

*****

The Green homestead was in Bulkara Road, Bellevue Hill. A small fleet of police vehicles lined both sides of the Road, centred on the scene of Elizabeth Green's murder. Greta passed a policeman at the front gate and walked down the path to the open front door. Just inside, she saw Luke Brand in deep conversation with someone in a white all-in-one forensic suit. Luke looked in her direction and nodded, and she moved towards him.

"The study is this way," he said, pointing over Greta's right shoulder. As they walked towards the study Greta asked, "Have you located Chalmers?"

"Not yet. He's not at his home. I wouldn't be surprised if he owned other properties. We're trying to figure out where. If he does have others, I don't expect they'll be in his name. He won't have made them easy to find. I'm still not sure what we'll achieve by … I mean we haven't got much to go on just yet."

"Maybe he'll have the bike with him, who knows? But, if nothing else, we'll be pissing him off. You know, Elizabeth Green said something interesting to me on the phone. Apart from identifying Chalmers." Greta caught Luke's eye and went on. "She said that Chalmers had built a mansion somewhere in a national park using the proceeds of the Green's pay-out to protect Brad. That could be one of the places he might have gone."

They entered the study. It was immediately familiar, the desk and bookshelves recognisable although the perspective from the doorway was not the one that had been captured by the artist. Books and papers were strewn around the floor, the desk drawers were all opened. No doubt, Chalmers' team had been looking for something. Greta walked in, along the wall to her right towards the artist's viewpoint. Greta felt a chill travel through her neck and back; this was undoubtedly the room that Angie's painting had portrayed.

Luke continued their conversation. "He can't have built anything *in* a national park."

"Sure, Luke, not inside one. Don't be so literal. But something right alongside would be a pretty attractive place to live in retirement."

Greta took in the art on the walls. They seemed to have been recently moved or handled, sitting unevenly on the walls, and she had an overwhelming desire to straighten them. She couldn't see the work from Angie's painting, the little one with people wearing masks that Mark Lewis had made such a fuss about. But, even to her untrained eye, the paintings that were hanging conveyed an impression of class.

"Did she say which national park?" asked Luke. "I mean, there's a shitload of national parks just in New South Wales."

"I don't think she did. And she ended the call seconds later. But he would have been paid off in or around June 2010. So, we can look at land purchases around that time. Big houses being bought or maybe built around late 2010, 2011. Thereabouts. We could choose areas close to some national parks and check for land sale records and building approvals."

Greta took out her phone and signalled to Luke that she wanted to take some photographs. Since this was not the scene of Elizabeth Green's murder, he waved his approval as he continued their conversation. "Chalmers won't have bought the house in his own name, Greta. It'll be hidden. And deep."

"Yeah, but the sale and approvals will still be there irrespective of the names he used. And I don't reckon he'll have built too far out of Sydney. I'll get people onto this at the crack of dawn."

She moved from work to work, noting the names and taking photographs. Where, according to Angie's painting, the little painting of the four people had hung—the one Mark had insisted depicted both the artist and his lover—a painting of a tan brown butterfly now hung. There was no signature, but the intense gloss surface was so reflective that it was difficult to capture an image from almost any angle. She beckoned Luke towards her to shield the painting from the light and she took a clearer photograph.

"Which people will you get onto this, Greta? Fraud squad people?"

Greta smiled. "Fair enough, Luke. No. The podcaster—Lisa—and her team do this sort of thing all the time. And I am in contact with them, so I'll get *them* to do it. It'll be a lot quicker than getting your staff to."

"So, you do know where Lisa Dimopoulos is?"

"I do, Luke, but I think she is safest being off the grid completely. I realise it's not the way you'd usually do things. But I've got this one, OK?"

Luke regarded Greta, a hint of a smile appearing. "What's she like, Greta?"

"Pretty bloody terrific, to be honest."

"I figured as much. Look after her, then."

Greta took one last photo of the study desk, exactly from Angie Richards' vantage point, a flash of reflected light marking the location of the butterfly painting. "That's the plan."

*****

Lisa called her team to action starting with text messages just before dawn. They'd all responded within half an hour, and the search for land purchases close to the boundaries of national parkland around Sydney from mid-2010 and for the next three years was launched.

On Greta's advice, Lisa arranged to check into a Bondi hotel under an assumed name; Greta retrieved some clothes and toiletries from Lisa's Paddington apartment before returning to pick her up from Midelton Road and delivering her to the hotel. Then she set off to work; it was going to require great effort to appear even partly engaged in her usual work duties.

*****

A cold sweat overcame Paul Lenzo as he saw the incoming call from Ray Chalmers. He detested the man and dreaded any contact he had to have with him; twice in one week was almost more than he could bear.

And he knew that this would have something to do with the noise surrounding the previous day's violence, the renewed interest in the Surry Hills fire and the whispers about that irregular inquiry from a member of the Fraud Squad less than a fortnight earlier. He'd not met Greta McCartney, but, inside his team, she'd been singled out as the original source of the renewed interest in the fire and was presumed to be connected to the proposed podcast.

"Hi Ray, how're things?"

"Good thanks Paul. I need some more information and I need it quickly. I think there's someone inside New South Wales police who is driving the podcast that intends to get the Surry Hills fire investigation re-opened. I think there's someone drip-feeding police intel to the media and that it's all linked in some way to the killing of that man Green yesterday and his mother last night. I know them—knew them—from my time as Assistant Commissioner. As much as it was possible, I regarded them as friends."

"Ray, the entire force is preoccupied with those killings. No one's got any time for the fire or the podcast. I can ask around, for sure, but there's only one issue here at the moment and it's not the one you're inquiring about."

The silence was long and absolute.

"Ray, are you still there?"

"Paul. I will not ask this again. And please don't think you can bullshit me. There's a female officer feeding information to the podcaster, and I want her name. You can tell it to me now or sometime in the next hour. Have you got that?"

Paul Lenzo knew that Chalmers was giving him a small lifeline, an opportunity to save face and redeem himself. It would also give him time to collect his thoughts. "I'll call you back, on this number, inside the hour."

"Thank you, Paul." And Chalmers hung up.

Lenzo closed his eyes and considered the fork in the road at which he now stood. Chalmers was getting old, but he could still expose Lenzo and ruin his life, not just his career. On the other hand, feeding the name of a colleague to a ruthless bastard like Chalmers, exposing her to intimidation and violence, would be a dog act. He understood – it was his career, his life; or hers.

Paul Lenzo knew it was inconceivable that Ray Chalmers was concerned about the loss of the Greens. In fact, he was well known to despise the very businesspeople with whom he had collaborated. Paul wondered what was so important about this fire that it had triggered this series of killings? What had Chalmers done that he was so keen to suppress?

He checked the internal list of police phone numbers and dialled.

"Fraud Squad, Raelene speaking."

"Hi Raelene, it's Paul Lenzo from Arson. Is Greta McCartney in?"

"Just one minute."

Lenzo waited and was soon connected.

"Greta McCartney speaking."

"Hi Greta, this is Paul Lenzo from Arson Squad. You rang us about two weeks back inquiring about the 2010 Surry Hills fire. At that stage, we had no additional information. I'm sure you know that one of the people we interviewed in that investigation was killed yesterday in Annandale. Bradley Green. And his mother was murdered last night as well. It's caused quite a stir, of course."

"How can I help you, Paul?"

Paul exhaled. "I just wanted to tell you that we are re-opening the investigation. Of course, things here are all focused on yesterday's killings right now. But there's been lots of … high-level interest … in the possible links between all these events. And that whole strange thing about a podcast. Did you catch that development?"

"I did, for sure. I'm interested in that high-level interest though. I know you can't be specific, but is that current or former high-level, or both?"

Lenzo almost smiled in relief. She was sharp. "Mostly former. They'll find out more or less everything pretty soon, you know, they always do."

"So true. It was really good of you to check back in with me. Thank you, Paul."

Paul ended the call. He waited the full hour before calling Ray Chalmers back and giving him Greta McCartney's name.

*****

Although there were a number of potential matches for the Chalmers' property, one stood out. It was a 2,000 square metre block at the end of an unnamed road near Mulgoa at the eastern edge of the Blue Mountains National Park, off Mulgoa Road north of the Mulgoa Township. It had been purchased in October 2010 by a company known as Calibre Pty Ltd. A search of that company had identified its sole director as the Bolt Action Trust; this led to a series of other companies and trusts but there was no individual name that could be pinned to the acquisition of this piece of land.

Likewise, the subsequent approval for building at that site, granted in June 2011 by the Penrith City Council, could not be traced to any individual person's name. A number of other purchases close to this and other national parks met the criteria they'd set, save for the fact that the people and entities who'd purchased or built on them were readily identified on the documents. The one that stood out was just north of Mulgoa. Greta picked up her phone and rang Luke Brand.

"Hi Gret, what's news?"

"Lisa's team have found a strong lead on Chalmers' second property. Google Earth shows a large house in a modern style, right on the edge of the Blue Mountains National Park. It's a two thousand square metre property, purchased in 2010 and the building approved in 2011. At the end of a road that doesn't even have a name."

"And it belongs to him?" asked Luke.

"Can't tell. Everything is in the name of some company or trust. We've followed them as far as we can, but it's all been set up to obscure who owns it and who built it. In my opinion, the deception is telling. I think we should regard this as the spot."

They both knew the clock was ticking.

"Great work, Gret. You keep your head down, my friend. I'll sort this end out."

*****

In the mix of emotions that occupied Ray Chalmers' thoughts, anger was easily the most prominent. He was appalled that a junior colleague, a woman and a failed member of the Major Crime Squad was at the heart of this betrayal. In Ray's mind, the bond between police officers was sacrosanct; their loyalty to each other, regardless of the circumstances, the bedrock of any effective police force.

He would have been incensed had this happened to any of his colleagues. That it now threatened his legacy and his liberty was cause for decisive action, for punishment as much as prevention. Maybe, Ray thought, he could not avoid being named in public, his reputation tarnished, his actions exposed and punished. But he was prepared to do whatever it took to silence this unworthy pest.

He called Danny Finnerty.

*****

From her conversation with Paul Lenzo, Greta understood that her role in events was now known to Ray Chalmers or very soon would be. She and those in her immediate vicinity would be at risk. Luke agreed with that assessment, and they formulated a plan. If they could apprehend Chalmers before he struck, the bikies would see no point in pursuing any further action and this would likely defuse the situation.

A lot rested on their shared conviction that the Mulgoa property was Chalmers' and that it was there that he was hiding away. And where they hoped to find compelling evidence, maybe even the motorbike used in Brad Green's murder.

It was already late morning when Luke Brand messaged Greta: *"Everything is in place. It's time to get going. Call as soon as you're on the Great Western."*

Greta got into the car and connected her phone to the blue tooth. It was an unmarked police vehicle with a few additional security features. She familiarised herself with the dashboard layout, loaded the route to the Mulgoa property and set off towards the edge of the Blue Mountains National Park. She called Lisa first. "How are you feeling?"

"I'm doing fine. Bored in this bloody hotel of course. But … as you requested, maintaining a low profile."

"I'm just on my way to Mulgoa to pick up our man. The Major Crime Squad is helping so I've got plenty of backup. I'll call you as soon as it's all tidied up."

"Tidied up? Are you kidding me? You don't think the bikies will be there to protect this guy?"

Greta bit her lip. "Lise, the bikies wouldn't get involved in a shoot-out with anyone but a rival gang. They're too smart to engage the police force directly. It's all about one man, OK?"

"You keep me in the loop, please. I am scared shitless for you."

"I know. I'm thinking of you too. Don't forget that these people are … that you also need to be careful. Stick to the rules, please. But call me if it's urgent."

Greta hung up, glanced in her rear-view mirror and checked the route map on her screen. She had an hour of driving ahead of her. She called Luke Brand. "Hi Luke. I'm just on the Great Western Highway. Where are you up to?"

"The drone team is preparing to launch over the property. I have another team approaching the turn-off on Mulgoa Road. They'll set up about two or three hundred metres from the corner, somewhere they can find cover. I think Chalmers will have his friends out looking for you already. Do you think you're being followed?"

"It's hard to tell, really. I keep looking. It might be clearer when I get off the Highway. Can I let the folk in Perth head back home?"

"Honestly, this will probably be all over in another hour or two. It's Helen and Pat O'Beirne who are at most risk. I think the others should be OK. Can you get them all to just stay put for a few more hours?"

"I'll ask. Keep me posted."

"Will do. And you too, please."

*****

Aresh had decided not to stay home but headed to work as usual. Cancelling his clinical duties would have been greeted with dismay by the clerical staff who would have had to re-arrange his clinic. He also knew he would be letting down a swag of patients. His junior colleagues, on the other hand, were generally happy to press on with a little less supervision.

Mostly, however, he realised he would be safer at work than at home. He only had a laptop to take with him and he set off for work around seven am.

His phone rang just as he pulled into his hospital parking spot.

"Hello Greta."

"Hi Aresh, I'm driving so I'll be quick. I've just sent you and Mark some photos from the Greens' study. It's the same place as the painting for sure. But the little painting that pointed him to the Greens in the first place isn't there. See what you all think. We hope we'll have things wrapped up here in a couple of hours. It is probably safe enough for you all to head out, but we think it'd be best if you stayed put for just a little while longer. It's probably Helen who is at most risk. I don't think they have your name or Mark's."

"I'm OK here," he said, catching a guilty glimpse of himself in his rear-view mirror and closing his eyes. "Can you tell me what's happening?"

"Not really, but we do have a key suspect and it's him we are about to … apprehend. If we do, we think the threat of more attacks will be over—or at least reduced—and it'll be more like routine police work from thereon in."

"I hope you do. Look after yourself, Greta. And let me know what's up as soon as you can."

*****

"Yes Danny?"

"We picked her up as she was leaving police headquarters just after eleven. She's in an unmarked cop car. That tells me that she anticipated she'd be followed. And I reckon she'll have help."

"I don't doubt that she'll be prepared. She's been smart all along. Can you say where you think that help will be? Do you know where she might be heading?"

"Right now, Ray, she's heading west on the M4, just past Parramatta."

Chalmers' eyes narrowed. "She's coming here. The cunning bitch. They think they're going to arrest me," thinking out loud more than conversing with the bikie chief. "She's still about thirty minutes away, no?"

"You should know. We could delay her, but I think there'll be other cops heading your way. If they're not there already."

Chalmers made his way up the stairs and into his bedroom as he continued the conversation with Danny Finnerty. "Can you pass her and get here first?"

"Easy." He signalled to Earl in the driver's seat who indicated right straight away and crossed into the outside lane, speeding up immediately.

Chalmers went out onto the bedroom balcony that looked out onto the national park. He looked skywards as he spoke. "Look out for police, Danny. They want to catch you as well, so you're just scouting now, OK? Do not take her out and do not engage with the police. And don't come off Mulgoa Road where we planned. If you haven't seen them by then, that'll tell me they're hiding on the approach road. Drive past the approach road and head right at the next turn-off. It's called Mayfair Road. Go to the end of Mayfair Road and I'll meet you there."

He gazed into the clouds above his house and watched carefully.

"Got that, Ray. What'll you do with the bike?"

The buzz of a drone he thought he'd heard was still faint but was now unmistakeable above his house. "I'll bring it to you and Earl. Right now, I've got a drone to deal with and then I'll be on the move. Let me know what you see and tell me exactly when you pass the turn-off. I'll meet you at the end of Mayfair Road with the bike."

*****

Mark and Linda looked through the images of the Green's study Greta had sent through. There was a wonderful Sali Herman, a Paddington Street scene, dated '46. Alongside it was a portrait by Louis Kahan of a strikingly beautiful woman perhaps in her thirties, a look of unbridled triumph in her eyes. On the adjoining wall was a still life painting of fruit in a shallow bowl atop a pedestal standing on a table, signed but not dated by Desiderius Orban. A fourth painting next to it was by Judy Cassab, an abstracted street scene, dated 1953, as beautiful a work as he had ever seen by the artist. All four artists had been European born and all were Jewish. All had emigrated to and settled in Australia, and all were now dead.

The fifth painting was the odd one out. Where he had hoped to see a work by Horace Brodzky, was a work of undoubted distinction which, after a quick search, he confirmed was by a living artist, the award-winning Sam Leach. Leach was represented by the Sydney gallery, Sullivan and Strumpf, based in Zetland. Mark had followed the exhibitions of this gallery's artists over many years but didn't know the proprietors in person.

"The Leach is a recent acquisition compared to the others. There's a theme in this small collection of works, I think, and the butterfly painting doesn't quite fit. It was exhibited in 2007. I wonder if he moved the Brodzky and bought the Leach to replace it?"

Linda put her arm around his shoulders and gave him a quick and gentle hug. "Sweetheart. The Greens might have bought any or even all of those paintings in the last twelve months. I'm not sure what message Angie Richards was trying to convey in her painting. It's clear that this study is where she depicted herself as the victim of rape perpetrated by Brad Green. And I think we all accept that there's a real connection between the Greens and Horace Brodzky. Maybe there was a painting by Brodzky in that study when Angie made her painting, and she included it to help identify the location. But maybe it never existed. Whatever else is true, there's no painting like that little Brodzky in that study now, OK?"

Mark Lewis shook his head. What had Angie really seen on the study wall?

*****

Greta had begun to believe that the white van she could see in her rear-view mirror was following her. Certainly, it had maintained a safe distance from her with no attempt to overtake her even when she'd intentionally slowed down a little. Until just after Parramatta, when it moved to the outer lane, sped up and passed her. She tried to see who was in the car as it overtook her, but traffic intervened. It had accelerated away and was soon out of sight. She continued to scan her mirror for alternative suspects. Her phone rang.

"Luke here. Any sign of a tail?"

"Nothing definite. There was a van that seemed to fit the bill, but it's just overtaken me and disappeared. I'm still suspicious though. I'd noticed it behind me for almost twenty K before it took off."

"Hmm. Keep a look-out. Nothing's changed here. And there's nothing happening at the house. We haven't seen him yet. We're assuming he's still inside. To be honest, we're assuming quite a bit."

"Maybe that van followed me long enough to be confident I was heading to Mulgoa. They might be setting up an ambush. Or going to Chalmers place to collect the bike."

"Yep. I've got teams in place to deal with them if that's what they're planning. If they go to Chalmers' place, we'll intercept them. Stick to your plan and let me know if you think anything's off."

*****

Chalmers retraced his steps through his house, descending the staircase, two flights down to the basement. He crossed the main room, past the table-tennis table and opened the door into the basement below the garage. Old pieces of machinery, a wall covered in tools and a solid worktable occupied most of the space. Below the worktable was a heavy metal container, secured by a lock with a six-digit code that contained his rifles and handguns.

He entered the code and opened the trunk, removing his Winchester Model 70 rifle. The ammunition cartridges were kept separately, and he opened the table drawer; a false partition made the drawer appear shallower than it was but, opened to its full length, he arrived at the rear compartment where he kept the ammunition. He took the cartridges he needed, closed the drawer and the trunk and set the rifle and ammunition on the tabletop. He then ascended the spiral staircase to the double-garage.

The garage had room for two large vehicles. Closest to the house was his Range Rover; next to it stood the Harley Davidson motorcycle used in Brad Green's murder, covered by a tarpaulin. He removed and folded the sheet and used the remote to open the garage door by no more than half a metre. He turned on the bike's ignition and its engine roared to life; he revved the engine for a few seconds and turned it off again.

Chalmers then headed out of the garage and back down the staircase, collected his rifle and ammunition and retraced his steps to re-enter the house. Just as he was about to run back up the stairs to his bedroom, he checked himself and strode quickly into his study. In a minute, he emerged with a self-satisfied smile on his face, and he sprinted up the stairs. Back in his bedroom, he loaded the rifle and approached the balcony. His timing and accuracy would need to be close to perfect. He called Danny. "Where are you? Have you seen anyone?"

"No sign of any police, Ray. We're just taking the slip road off the M4 to Mulgoa Road. Probably ten to fifteen minutes from the pick-up point. It's Mayfair Road that we're heading for, right?"

"Yep, that's the one. I'll meet you at the end of Mayfair." He finished the call and turned his phone on silent. He stood in the doorway onto the balcony and listened again. The drone was barely audible but, as best he could judge, it was situated to the east of his house, heading towards him. The balcony faced west onto the national park so it would pass overhead with little opportunity for Chalmers to gauge its height and velocity before it identified him; it would be like hunting a bird and he knew he would be punished severely if he failed with his first shot or two.

The drone approached, the sound of its whirring propellers ever louder. He glimpsed a view of it, perhaps twenty metres overhead and took a solitary step out onto the balcony. He aimed the rifle skywards, located the drone and in a smooth and practised fashion locked in on his target and obliterated it with his first shot.

He picked up the spent cartridge as drone debris fell from above, some of it into his yard. He re-entered the house, closed the balcony door and headed for the garage at pace. Once there, he opened the garage door, fired up the motorcycle and drove out into the daylight, closing the garage door behind with the remote. He hoped that he would be out of sight for long enough to complete his escape.

*****

"We've lost all drone vision. I think it's been taken out. It was directly over the house when everything went black. We're all flying blind right now."

"Shit, Luke. Do you think Chalmers shot it down?" asked Greta.

"I think that's what's happened. Probably just to tell us he knows we're here. But maybe to buy some time while he moves around. There's only one way in and out by road, and he won't get far on foot in the bush around that house."

"Has that white van appeared yet?"

"No sign of it. How about you? Any new tail?"

"Nothing here. I'm just approaching the turn-off to Mulgoa. I don't suppose you have a second drone you can use?"

"Not here. Honestly, Gret, I didn't think this would happen."

Greta glided into the slip lane and decelerated on approach to Mulgoa Road. There was little traffic to contend with and she turned left, heading south-west and then south through Penrith. "I'd get your team into that house as soon as you can. If that van was ever tailing me in the first place, they're not going to be interested any more. Get there now, Luke. We need to find that bike."

"Fair call. You get here quick, too, OK?"

*****

Ray Chalmers had walked the bush around his home scores of times. He'd fashioned a sealed driveway which ran from the approach road and curved past his front door and then sharp right past the entrance to the garage, almost encircling his home. It connected to an unsealed track into bush to the west of his property. He drove the bike along this track now, past a small, isolated household nestled amongst some trees, before it turned east towards the Glendon family property with its tennis court and massive homestead.

At this point, he left the track and drove through bush, picking up other unsealed pathways in a criss-cross fashion and avoiding the ponds and puddles that formed each winter. He manoeuvred his heavy bike in a roughly southerly direction across a few hundred metres of bushland. Not far from the end of Mayfair Road, the bush thinned out and he passed close to the Rankin property, unoccupied as usual for the winter months, and out onto the sealed road. Danny and Carlos were waiting for him in the van.

Within sixty seconds, they'd loaded the bike, and Chalmers handed over the rifle and the spent cartridge. "Get that rifle back to my home in Balmain. Shirley will be expecting it. And you need to hide this bloody bike properly or get rid of it altogether."

Danny nodded and within seconds the van had disappeared back in the direction of Mulgoa Road. Ray Chalmers turned and retraced his pathway through the bush, this time on foot. The onset of rain brought another smile to his face. The heavier the better he thought.

*****

Despite the downpour, Greta drove just above the speed limit until the turn-off to the house she now felt certain belonged to Chalmers. She couldn't quite piece things together but the feeling that she'd been outsmarted gnawed away at her. Was that white van part of this, maybe even just to distract her, or had it been a mere coincidence? Why had Chalmers shot down the drone, if that's what had happened?

It was just over a kilometre from the turn-off to the house. As she drove west, windscreen wipers at maximum speed, weathered and barely legible signs foretold the approach of *Notre Dame*, the once-dazzling headquarters of a bogus charity and private zoo, now abandoned and derelict. Greta felt crushed by a feeling of impending defeat.

She knew that the consequences for her and Lisa's safety would be serious if they could not implicate Ray Chalmers; but it was the prospect of failing Lisa that made Greta feel most hollow. She tried to push those thoughts away as her car approached the small crowd of police that had gathered outside a large house on the left-hand side of the road. The weary body language of that group suggested they'd been foiled; she knew it augured badly for the news they would soon give her. She pulled up just past the house.

Luke Brand walked towards her car, a rain jacket protecting him from the easing rain, his hoody pulled over his head. "The bike's not here. At least not anymore. I'm pretty sure it was in the garage but there's not much to find. Any tyre tracks have been washed away." He waved in the direction of the sky, wordlessly apportioning blame. "I'm waiting for forensics to go over things in detail."

"Is Chalmers here?"

"Yeah. He turned up on foot, as if out of nowhere, a few minutes after we got here. Says he was just out for a stroll in the bush when the heavens opened.

He's inside. He's cooperating. There's no sign of a rifle, not even in his safe. I'm heading in to interview him now. Perhaps you'd better stay away."

"He knows who I am, Luke, I might as well sit in. He'll have had people following me. I think that white van was a tail after all but, as soon as he figured out that I was coming here, he called it off. Maybe they came to collect the bike?"

"Maybe. We didn't see a thing along this road. He's a slippery bastard. Let's go inside."

They walked through the front door of the house, Greta noting the western-facing aspect of the house with its abundance of full-length glass taking in the view of the forest. Her phone vibrated and she saw that it was Lisa. "You go on Luke. I have to take this."

"Hi Lise, are you ok?"

"That's what I wanted to ask you. What's happened? Have you got him?"

Greta sighed. She found a door off the main hallway and entered what was, she imagined, Ray Chalmers' study. There was a small but solid desk with a large computer screen on it, a bank of filing cabinets against the wall behind the desk, to her right, with a long, high window facing out onto the driveway above it. Paintings were dotted on the walls to her left and in front of her, low shelves on both walls housing books and a few small sculptures. Quite the collector, Greta thought. "Yes, we're interviewing him now."

She approached the painting to her left as she gathered her thoughts, fearful of their conversation. It was a neat painting of a house and buildings that looked as if they might be farm buildings. Signed "R Wakelin 48". Maybe she'd take some photos of these as well?

"Can I get out of this hotel now?" Lisa's tone sounded tense and irritable.

"Yes, it's almost time to head home. I'll let the others know too. Let me pick you up when I'm finished here. We can go back to my place. It's being watched so we'll be safe. I'll take you home to Paddington as soon as I get the all-clear. I'm bound to have some paperwork to get through, so I might not get to the hotel until about six. Can you stay put until then?"

"Why do you still need your house watched?"

Greta's shoulders dropped. On the wall in front of her was another painting, a simple arrangement employing distinct blocks of colour. In it, a road passed through rolling green-yellow pastures beneath a bright blue sky, a glimpse of the ocean settling the scene as coastal. It was signed in its lower right "Rah Fizelle". It was beautiful, she thought. "I think they'll be gone tomorrow. I'll give you the whole story as soon as I pick you up."

They said their goodbyes and Greta placed the phone on the desk. She sat on its edge, her back to the study door, gazing again at the Fizelle in front of her. In her desire to impress Lisa, she had exposed this unanticipated lover to life-threatening risk. She could now see that she had not been able to secure Lisa's safety; or her own. She could only imagine the pleasure Ray Chalmers would take in pursuing them both once he found out that they were an item.

She felt overwhelmed by a depressing sense of her unworthiness; that she did not warrant Lisa's love or trust; that she should never have imagined she might. She had to end the relationship now, before it became too serious, before Lisa figured out for herself how ordinary Greta really was. It was the right thing to do for Lisa, the only practical way she might help her. Unless, of course, Lisa had already reached the same conclusion.

Wakelin's farmhouse to her left looked down on her, she imagined, with stern reproach. She looked forwards again, but Fizelle's road was heading away from her, fleeing towards the ocean, disappointed and disapproving. She eased herself off the edge of the desk and turned towards the study door knowing she had to join Luke in his interview, dreading having to face Ray Chalmers.

The wall alongside the door harboured another painting, an Aboriginal motif she thought, white dots on a royal blue background. Unsigned. It was framed behind glass but was hung unevenly and it sat lower on the wall than seemed right. It looked as if it had been both chosen and hung in a rush. Even to Greta's untrained eye, it was out of keeping with the other paintings and its haphazard placement was inconsistent with what she knew about Ray Chalmers. She approached the painting, restraining herself from straightening it. Whatever significance its incongruous appearance in this room held escaped her. She knew she was delaying her confrontation with Chalmers.

In the corner of her eye, on the floor to her left, poking out from behind the filing cabinet that fitted neatly into the corner of the study, she caught a glimpse of the reverse side of a small painting. She was drawn towards it, surprised by the strength of the curiosity that she felt. Greta felt as if she almost floated the few short steps towards the wall before she knelt down, easing the painting out from between wall and cupboard to inspect it more closely. At the top of the backing board she saw a stamp from "Heinemann publishers and editorial offices, 15-16 Queen Street Mayfair". In old-fashioned type print, it was addressed to:

Horace Brodzky, Esq. 37 Oxford Road N.W.6

Below it, written in pencil, was:

Horace Brodsky
The Masked Ball
Oil on Board Signed H Brodsky '34

She slipped on some disposable gloves and picked it up, her heart racing. Turning it over she saw four characters she recognised in an instant. "Horace Brodzky '34" was painted neatly in the lower right corner, smaller than, but otherwise exactly as, in Angie's painting. What was it doing here?

Elizabeth Green's last words reverberated in Greta's head: "robbed us of a family treasure". Mark Lewis had been right about the painting after all. This had been a gift to Sam Green from his aunt—her name was Rachel, Greta recalled—who had been a close friend of Brodzky. This lovely little creation was that treasure, a family heirloom that had been part of the price Chalmers had extracted from the Greens.

An unexpected and overwhelming surge of emotion rose in Greta's chest. She rang Mark Lewis using the video facility on What's App.

Mark answered. "Hello, Greta? It's nice to see you. Is everything OK?"

She could see Linda sitting next to him and glimpses of their hotel room in the background. "Yes and no. But I have something to show you. I'm in the home of the man we suspect has coordinated these killings. He is cooperating with police, mostly because he knows we don't have much evidence against him I'm sorry to say. I'm in his study and this was on the floor."

Greta rotated her phone to show Mark the Brodzky painting which she had placed on the desk. She could hear his intake of breath but continued. "I spoke to Elizabeth Green, just before she was murdered, and she told me about the money this man had extorted from her. But she also said that he had robbed them of a family treasure. I think that this painting is that treasure and that it is somehow the proof of that awful deal. But I'm not sure what to do next."

"Do you have some gloves with you?"

"Yes, I've got them on."

"Can you turn it over and show me what's on the back?"

Greta set the phone down and turned the painting over. She showed Mark what had been written there.

"The Masked Ball" whispered Mark.

There was a lengthy silence.

"Mark, please, I need your help."

"Sorry, sorry. That's … incredible."

"What sort of record of purchase would this guy have?"

"Hmm. I suppose he could simply say that he was gifted the work. But that would only invite questions about who had gifted it to him. He could just say it was the Greens. Or maybe name someone else. Even then, whoever he had got it from would have to have their own records of how and when they'd acquired it."

"I don't really follow you. I don't think he would risk mentioning the Greens, do you?"

"When I think about it Greta, I don't think this is the sort of work anyone would gift to anyone else except by inheritance. It's a rare work by a special artist. No collector in their right mind would give it away and this man who's now got it would know that. I really think he'll have documents that vouch for its acquisition. And bank records that support the payment."

"But those documents will be fakes, won't they?"

"I'm not sure he'd want to have faked them. I reckon he's forced Sam Green to sell it to him as part of the deal to help his son. The documentation will probably look like a straightforward transaction, and I suspect the price will be close to market price. That will connect him to the Greens, but I think that this crook of yours will simply have added that purchase price on to the pay-out for the protection. I doubt he ever expected he'd need to prove that he'd bought it fair and square, but I'd be surprised if he hadn't prepared for that possibility. Still, you never know. The documentation might not exist or might have been falsified."

"I found it on the floor and there's a painting on the wall nearby that looks like it's been put up in a rush." Greta showed Mark the Aboriginal painting and then the two other works that were hanging in the study.

"Yes. It seems as if he's taken the Brodzky down in a hurry, maybe after he saw the image of Angie's painting and recognised it. He clearly didn't want to attract any attention to the Brodzky even if he does have sound documentation."

"I agree. He probably didn't anticipate that we would be able to track him down to this house. I think you're right, that he is sensitive about the Brodzky and how he came to have it. I'm just not sure how this helps us."

"Whatever else is true, Greta, if this man has any documents about the acquisition of this painting, we both know that they won't reflect the exact nature of the transaction. Not for a minute do I believe that Sam Green would have willingly sold anyone this piece of his family's history. But I wouldn't be asking this suspect of yours for those documents straight up because, the moment you do, he'll catch on that we suspect he has the painting and Lord knows what he'll do to it."

"Do you think he might destroy it?"

"Who knows? But I agree with you that he's moved it in a hurry. And that means he suspects other people might regard it as evidence … of something. If he's the man behind these killings, he clearly hasn't hesitated to do a whole lot worse to protect his name, so I really don't think he'd think twice about getting rid of a painting, especially one he never even bought in the usual sense."

"OK. I'll photograph it and put it back where I found it."

"In fact, Greta, I wouldn't be talking to him about any of his paintings. Even that might make him suspicious you've seen the Brodzky. Do you have any good reason to interrogate the origins of all his possessions?"

"I think we do. We could query the size of his whole asset base and demand evidence of purchases and bank records – a complete audit of his possessions. And that should include any paperwork for the Brodzky painting, which might give us an avenue to explore."

Even as she spoke, Greta didn't feel like this was much of a plan. The raid on Chalmers' house had so far yielded little of value. Her conviction that they would surprise him and find some telling evidence had proven false. In truth, it had all boiled down to finding the bike. Chalmers knew he was in the spotlight, and he knew why. But that spotlight had revealed nothing except the Brodzky.

Greta told Mark she thought it was now safe for him and Linda to leave the hotel and asked him to let the others know as well. She signed off and replaced *The Masked Ball* on the floor, facing towards the filing cabinet, exactly as she had found it. It was such a diminutive object, yet it spoke of sweeping connections that traversed continents dating back almost a century.

She took a video of the study and, as she recorded, she narrated a brief account of what she could see on the walls and the floor. When she'd finished, Greta hesitated yet again. Her thoughts raced. Although they had failed to find any concrete evidence to implicate Ray Chalmers in any of the numerous crimes in which she believed he had been instrumental, something inside her, deep and persuasive, did not want this little painting left at the mercy of such a monster. For sure, he would notice that it was missing; he'd be angry that it had been stolen and acutely aware that its significance to the Greens and to these murders had been understood. But what would he do? Would he really risk bringing its disappearance to the attention of the police?

Greta took off her jacket, picked up *The Masked Ball* and used her jacket to wrap it up securely. She carried the hidden painting out to her car, the winter chill by the roadside catching her breath. Once the painting was safely concealed on her back seat, she put her jacket back on and returned inside to join Luke for what was left of the interview with Ray Chalmers. She knew that she had acted improperly, removing a potentially important piece of evidence; and that Chalmers would soon detect its absence and know that it had been her who had taken it.

*****

The police contingent had completed their first round of interviews, along with a search of his home and a forensic inspection of the garage. They'd retrieved the fragments of their drone many of which had fallen within his property but had not identified the weapon that, they presumed, had destroyed it. Chalmers knew that they'd be back, and Greta McCartney had made it clear they would be focusing on his assets and how he'd come to accumulate so many possessions. He'd found her presence at the interview—her entire involvement in this investigation, which was well outside her brief in the Fraud Squad—both intriguing and irritating.

Chalmers was confident that his paperwork would stand up to any police interrogation and knew that his lawyers would make the entire process laborious and exasperating for them. He felt calm and, as ever, in control.

As soon as the police had all left, he went to his study and sat down at his desk. He booted up his computer and opened his emails; there were pressing appointments to arrange. He leant back and surveyed his study.

Something felt out of balance, unfamiliar. He checked the layout of his desk, the position of his mousepad and his paper tray. He scanned the walls in front and to his right then turned back to his left. The painting alongside the door jumped out at him, its style and tone discordant. He exhaled in relief, remembering how he'd switched paintings earlier on, just as things were heating up.

He realised that he'd have to remove the Brodzky before the police returned. He doubted that anyone would connect it to the painting of Brad Green raping that artist and, in any event, he had complete documentation of its acquisition from Sam Green. But he did not want to attract any attention to it at all. He would no longer hang it—or store it—anywhere. It'd be safer to destroy it altogether. Shame, he thought. He'd got quite used to it.

Chalmers stood up and approached the dot painting. It didn't fit in this room and needed to be replaced. He straightened it and glanced down towards the Brodzky. It wasn't protruding from behind the filing cabinet as he recalled having left it and a quiver of unease passed through him. He walked towards the wall and peered into the gap between the wall and the cabinet. The space was empty.

He passed his left hand deep into the space and down towards the floor, his palm sliding down the cool wall, feeling for something that he could not see. He closed his eyes, trying to summon a memory of having placed the painting somewhere else, but he knew he'd put it there and he knew it had been taken.

"That fucking devil," he muttered to himself. His voice became louder, his house empty but his anger boiling over. "McCartney – you bitch!" How did she figure it out? She must have been in his study, snooping around, while Brand and those idiots were interviewing him. He yelled a series of expletives, incoherent and wild with anger, to no-one in particular. "She's tampered with evidence," he growled. "You fucking low life."

Chalmers stood up, steadying himself against his desk as his thoughts began to crystallise, his desire for retribution absolute. What could she do with it anyway, the stupid bitch? She'd have to hide the damn thing. She couldn't admit she'd taken evidence from a possible crime scene. White hot with rage, he sat at his desk, closed his eyes and forced himself to calm down. Then he called Danny Finnerty.

"Thanks for dropping off the rifle, Danny. Have you dealt with the bike?"

"Of course. We've made it disappear. How did you go with the cops?"

"Very well, in fact. They've got nothing on me, and I'll have them running around in circles for years trying to get me." He'd opened his top drawer, suddenly anxious that McCartney might have been there as well. Relieved, he felt for the small false compartment that contained the old metal cigarette lighter, unused for more than a decade, that he'd removed from police evidence and kept as a memento. "Funny thing is that the Greens were probably my only liability. Two of them are gone, and old man Sam's lost his marbles. There's a daughter and some grandkids, but I don't think they know much." He held his phone to his ear in his left hand and rolled the lighter around in his right, soothed by its smooth surface and its deft weight.

"Can we find out for sure, Ray? I'm feeling exposed here. I'd like us to be certain."

"That could be a bit tricky, Nails. I expect the police will be guarding the daughter pretty closely. If her old man made a record of his interactions with me, Carlos certainly didn't find any indication of that at the Green's house. The old man's desk was mostly empty anyway and the few thumb drives we retrieved contained nothing of note. The PC and the laptop he took had nothing in them about the fire. And Carlos was confident that Mrs Green knew nothing of any permanent record of those events."

Chalmers paused to emphasise the point. "I'm pretty sure the Greens wanted to keep it in the dark as much as me. I doubt the daughter knows anything about me and I'd be more than surprised if there's any evidence at all that points to me. The longer this goes on, the less likely it is that there's anything for us to worry about. I'd say you're safe."

He dwelt on that thought for a moment and put the lighter down on his desk. "I'd say *they're* stuffed."

"What about the painting? That's still in Perth and we haven't seen it. Is that something we need to sort out?"

"Nails, I've seen an image. The artist painted Brad Green raping her in his father's study. It was an attempt to expose Brad Green, but it was painted before she was killed, so it has no link to the fire. It's not worth raiding any more places to get hold of it. That painting is not a threat to us," he said between gritted teeth.

"And the podcaster and that McCartney woman we followed this morning? Should we still be worried about what they know?"

"Well, that's the main reason I've called you. I met her this afternoon, the policewoman, McCartney. She's a smart bitch, that's for sure. She and the podcaster are both dykes, you know, which is probably how they connected in the first place. They might even be a couple. I've no doubt McCartney's been feeding her podcaster friend information and keeping her one step ahead of us.

McCartney's the one that worries me, Danny. She's the threat we need to contain. I want to make her suffer, Danny. This'll be the last thing I ask of you."

Danny Finnerty listened and nodded as Ray Chalmers outlined his request. "Got that boss. They're still watching us closely, but I think we can sort that out."

Chalmers train of thought continued. "Thanks again for collecting the bike and the Winchester. That worked out very well."

"Our pleasure, Ray. As long as you're happy with how things sit, I'm happy too. We'll sort out McCartney and then we'll need to square things off. I'll be in touch in a day or two when I've calculated the tariff, OK?"

Having settled on a plan of action, Ray Chalmers anger was subsiding. He was, after all, more than OK. It had needed his expert marksmanship to take down the drone and his quick thinking to smuggle the bike and rifle out of sight. Then there was the rain that had obscured the motorbike's tracks. His skill and wits, combined with the heavens' intervention, had saved the day. He was convinced the gods were on his side, a sure indication that he remained worthy of their backing.

It was just that he'd be even more OK when Nails had secured the last piece of the puzzle. He headed down to his garage to attend to the lighter once and for all. There would be no more pleasure to be extracted from this small souvenir.

*****

"Are you back home?" Mark had called Pat O'Beirne as soon as he and Linda had settled back into their North Perth townhouse. He had just emailed Pat the images that Greta had sent him from Chalmers' Mulgoa study.

"Still a bit of a crime scene here," said Pat. "The police haven't quite finished with us. But we're pleased to be home and there'll be protection for a night or two. They don't seem to think the intruders will be coming back again."

"Glad to hear it. I've just emailed you some images. Greta sent them through a bit earlier."

Pat walked out of his lounge, where he'd been enjoying a quiet drink, and headed to his study. He caught Helen's eye as he walked past her and gestured to her to follow him. He turned on his laptop, switched his phone to speakerphone, and he and Helen pulled up chairs to look at the screen. Pat pushed back on his chair and reached around to close the study door.

"Have you got the email?"

"Just opening it now, Mark," as Pat rolled back to the desk.

Mark strummed the desk alongside his computer screen with his fingers, Linda beside him and their phone also on speaker. Linda placed her hand over Mark's to quell the nervous tapping. He looked at her and nodded slowly.

"OK, I'm looking at what you've called "number one"," said Pat. "That's a Sali Herman, right? Where is this from?"

"These next few images are taken from the Greens' study in Bellevue Hill early this morning. That *is* a Sali Herman. These are the paintings on the study walls. Image number two is a portrait we think is of Elizabeth Green painted by Louis Kahan."

There was silence on the phone that Mark recognised as the sound of Pat processing the information.

"Number three is a Cassab."

"What a ripper," said Helen, over Pat's shoulder.

"I know. And it's early. 1953. And number four is an Orban. That's a beauty too."

More silence. "Number five is the last image of a painting from the study. This is the spot where Angie had painted that small Brodzky."

"That's no Brodzky" said Pat, Mark detecting the confusion in his voice.

"No. It's a Sam Leach, painted in 2007. It's got a high gloss finish so it's a hard image to capture, but I've identified the work from his Sydney gallery's online records. It's definitely one of his. And the last photo Greta took, number six, is from the vantage point of the artist in Angie's painting. This is definitely the rape scene."

"For sure," said Helen. "But why did she paint in a Brodzky when there's something completely different there?"

"The Leach doesn't really fit in, Mark," said Pat. "The Brodzky made more sense. It would have completed a fine grouping of Jewish artists. But Leach?"

"No, it's definitely the odd one out although it looks like a wonderful painting to me. Let's keep moving. Image number seven was taken this morning, from this presumed criminal's outer Sydney home, the one they'd just raided. Greta hasn't told me who or exactly where." Before he could say anything more, there was a sharp collective indrawing of breath, loudest from Linda and Helen but also from Pat who emitted a sound that was part sigh, part groan.

"It's the Brodzky," Pat said, stating the obvious, staring at his screen.

"Oh my god," exclaimed Helen, "it really does exist."

"Yep, and it's found its' way to the home of the man who Greta believes extorted cash from the Greens to protect their son from being convicted of murdering Angie Richards. Greta is convinced that the painting became part of the same deal and now she's trying to gather evidence to prove it."

"How's she going to do that?" asked Pat. "He's bound to have documents that cover it all off."

"It makes me sick to think that he owns that little masterpiece. How does he say he got hold of it?" asked Helen.

"Well, that's the thing, Helen, I've advised Greta not to draw attention to the Brodzky just yet. Or any of his paintings. They're going to investigate all of his assets and they hope his records don't match with his account of how he came by so much … stuff. That's the plan, anyway."

Mark was waiting for Pat to express an opinion, but it was Linda who said what they were all thinking. "You mean that the way they hope to expose this man," she paused for a moment, "someone who might well have engineered three murders in one day, is by pointing out a discrepancy between documents surrounding his acquisition of a solitary painting?"

"I don't think they'll find anything that will help them," said Pat, adding to the gloom. "And if this man gets wind of this, he might well destroy that beautiful little Brodzky."

Mark broke the crushed silence. "Look, they know they're dealing with a very shrewd criminal. They're going to need to be thorough and persistent. I can't imagine it's going to happen quickly."

"So, are we all out of danger yet? Won't this man come after us again?" Helen's tone was shrill. "And what if the police can't find the link they need to convict him?"

"Has anyone inspected Sam Green's records?" asked Pat, seemingly undeterred by Helen's concerns. "Perhaps he left some pointer to what happened. It makes more sense to go through the original owner's paperwork than to look for some unlikely discrepancy in the criminal's."

"I don't honestly know, Pat. But I'll ask Greta as soon as we finish this call." Mark spoke to Helen. "She's confident that they won't be coming after any of us."

"OK, Mark. Let's assume we're all safe," said Pat. "You'd better let Aresh know. And Cathy too, I suppose. I need to think about all of this – something doesn't quite fit."

Mark assured them he would let the others know straight away and closed the call. He sat back in his study chair, turned to face Linda and spoke. "Do you think they still want to get hold of Angie's painting?"

"That image is now in everyone's hands, darling. I don't think getting hold of the painting itself would make any difference at all. It's Greta who I think's most in danger. This guy knows who she is and doesn't seem the sort of person to leave things be. I think you should call her now. Pat might be right. Maybe Sam Green did leave some papers that could help her."

*****

The traffic on the Great Western Highway was heavy and Greta's thoughts were dark. She'd texted Lisa as she left Chalmers' property to say she'd be about an hour and a half. She couldn't face speaking to her about how little they had against Chalmers. And now the trip looked like it would take even longer.

Waves of self-recrimination washed over her, exposing her life as one that seemed to her to have been spent disappointing the people she most loved; never quite meeting expectations, her own ambitions and relationships forever evaporating in front of her own eyes; destined to be alone. She imagined Lisa sitting in the hotel's lobby, impatient, distressed and angry.

Getting back to the Eastern Suburbs in this congestion would be arduous. Still, once it was done, she would be able to retreat inside her lacklustre cocoon in Midelton Road and back inside the Fraud Squad, where she would, on her own again, set about arresting yet another decline in her prospects in life. For now, she would have to put the self-reproachment on hold; any analysis of the hubris that had led her to this debacle to be deferred, at least until she had made Lisa safe.

Her phone rang and she was shaken back to reality. It was Mark Lewis. "Hi Mark."

"Hi Greta. How are you?"

"I'm OK. What's up?"

"You're still in the car?"

"Yes. On my way … back to Bondi."

"Give our best wishes to Lisa. How is she?"

"I'm about to find out, I suppose."

There was a pause before Mark spoke. "I showed all those images to Helen and Pat. They agreed that this man is likely to have perfectly credible records of a purchase of the Brodzky, but Pat is certain that Sam Green would also have kept some documentation. That material might be telling. You had a good look through Green's study, didn't you?"

"The study had been ransacked, but I don't think we've gone through the papers there in detail."

"Was anything taken?"

"I really don't know. I think the investigating team are meeting up with Sam and Elizabeth Green's daughter, at the family home, tomorrow. She might know something. But you're right," she sighed, "it makes sense to go through the study in detail. What should we be looking for?"

"He might have left some records on a USB stick if they haven't all been taken, and there'll probably be hard copy records as well. Maybe an old-fashioned file with documents and photos, exhibition catalogues, correspondence from galleries or even artists. That sort of thing. Pat and I both think he'll have kept that sort of stuff somewhere."

"Sure, I'll ask Major Crime if I can go back again." But would she really know what she was looking at? Dejected, Greta felt the unmistakeable apprehension of impending disgrace. She recognised it well.

"Would it be of any help if Pat and I came across and went through it with you? I think we'd like to help out that much if we could. If you think that'd be alright with the police?"

Greta was caught by surprise at Mark's offer of help. "Yes, I would," she said, and, without warning, tears flooded her eyes. Thank goodness Mark couldn't see her, she thought. She sniffed. "I'll check with the head of the investigation and let you know. How soon can you be here?"

"I'll call Pat straight away and we'll book flights for tomorrow. It'll be nice to meet you all."

"I'll call you back. Thank you, Mark."

*****

Linda waited for Mark to summarise the conversation.

"I've offered to go over and help her sort through the paperwork there, looking for a clue to the Brodzky. I'm not sure I can really help but she sounded very down to me. I think she and Lisa might be … struggling."

"Ah! Mark Lewis to the rescue yet again. I think you should confine yourself to matters of art, Mr Lewis."

"Yes, of course. I know my limitations. I'm going to ask Pat to come with me. He'll pick things up that I miss."

"Two great experts in relationships, I don't think. Still, if you can find something that helps convict these evil people, you'll at least make Greta safe. It's a pity I can't join you to provide a bit of emotional support."

"For me as well. I just need to see for myself if there's anything there. I can't believe Sam Green would've let someone take that painting from him without keeping a record that would at least tell us more about the painting, even if he didn't describe how and why he had parted with it. Anyway, I'm probably clutching at straws, but I've got to take this as far as I can, or I'll never be satisfied."

"I get it, Mark. You're still hoping to prove that Brodzky painted his girlfriend. But please be careful about Greta and Lisa. Those sorts of things need plenty of space to sort themselves out." She gave him a quick hug and headed off to the bedroom. "It's been a strange day. You and Pat had better sort out your travel plans."

*****

Greta pulled up outside the hotel's front door. She could see Lisa slumped on a couch, her travel bag on the floor beside her. The car Greta was driving wasn't her own and Lisa had looked up and, not recognising it, had turned away, affording Greta a few more seconds to observe Lisa's tired posture and her lovely face. She had braced herself for a cool reaction and had prepared some lines to explain why, in her opinion at least, it would be in Lisa's best interests for them to take some time apart.

She got out of her car and entered the hotel. Lisa looked up, almost startled, and shot to her feet. She leapt at Greta and burst into tears. "Don't you ever do that again," she sobbed. "I've had visions all day of you being shot or bombed or God knows what. Greta," and she pulled back a few centimetres and clasped her surprised lover's cheeks, "I honestly thought you might not get back alive." And she kissed her on the lips, with passion and meaning.

For a moment, Greta felt unmoored, unable to respond. Her scripted lines had evaporated, and she'd not prepared any others on which she could now call. But the weight of Lisa's body in her arms infused her with a powerful sense of wellbeing and a confused mixture of lingering unworthiness and renewed hopefulness. "It wasn't quite as dramatic as you think." Greta searched Lisa's face for any hint of pretence. "Oh, shit. Lisa. I've put us both in danger. I'm just a fucking train wreck." And Greta started to cry, the two of them hugging and weeping, oblivious to their surroundings and, for a few seconds, unwilling to let each other go.

Chapter 27
Tuesday, 8 March 1938

The eight works on paper and the photographs had been laid flat, each separated by sheets of tissue paper, protected by numerous sheets of newspaper and surrounded by a makeshift plywood box held together by string. The little oil painting, however, had been wrapped in its own piece of cloth and secured with string in a manner that had also created a simple handle. These were Rachel's mementos, her memories of more than three years in London, in the company of Horace Brodzky – artist, writer, drinking partner, lover.

Rachel set the box down in her cramped cabin. She unwrapped the painting, laid it on the narrow bed and gazed at its characters once again. It had been completed shortly before she'd first met Horace and, of all his works, it remained her favourite. She'd even met Mark Gertler, one of Horace's many friends from in and around the Café Royal, who he had depicted in the painting's background. Most of all, it was the fact that Horace had painted himself in it that appealed to her.

She'd left her departure until the latest possible date, the clamouring drums of war and her parents' strident wishes convincing her to depart. She planned to return to London as soon as possible but who knew what the coming months might bring? If there was war, as her father insisted there would be, she wondered if she would ever get to return. And, when she did, would London—and Horace—still be the same?

Chapter 28
Wednesday, 14 June 2023

"What are you going to do with it? You can't leave it here, on your wall."

"I'm not sure."

"Oh my god, Greta. He's going to send someone to look for it, we all know that. And they'll come here first."

"He might not notice that it's missing. At least not straight away."

Lisa held her girlfriend in a cool stare, lowering her voice for emphasis. "He will already know that it's been taken. He'll know it was you. He'll want it back."

"Yes, yes and no. I promise, I'm not burying my head in the sand. OK, so he will figure it out quickly. But I'm not sure he'll want to get it back so much as to get rid of it completely. It's me that he probably wants to get to. Jesus, though, Lise, it's a beautiful painting, isn't it?"

The two women approached it, standing shoulder to shoulder no more than forty centimetres from its surface. "That's Brodzky," said Lisa pointing to the character with the moustache on the left.

"And that's the one Mark insists is Rachel Blazov, Sam Green's aunt," added Greta referring to the unmasked female character to Brodzky's left. Brodzky was pointing towards her and, like the two other characters, he also appeared to be looking at her. Only the unmasked woman looked directly at the viewer, her expression unfathomable but somehow defiant. "It's hard to believe it was painted ninety years ago."

"You can't leave it here, Gret."

"That's the whole thing. I *have* to leave it here. If they do come looking for it, as you say, this is where they'll come first and, if they get inside, I'd rather they found it quickly than tear the place to shreds looking for it. Or go on a rampage elsewhere. To be honest, I'm not sure he'll want to draw anyone's attention to this painting. He knows I can't hand it in to the Major Crime Squad, or even return it to the Greens, while he remains free. I'd be admitting to tampering with evidence at a possible crime scene. If he still had it, I'm sure he'd have gotten rid of it. At least here, the painting is relatively safe."

Lisa shook her head and a wry smile formed on her face, acknowledgement of having lost the argument. "I'm having a shower. The girls are coming around to help me clear out the Lieb's garage and we'll be gone by nine. I'll get them to drop me off at home and I can drive to work from there. Be careful, Greta. And give my best wishes to Mark and Pat."

*****

Bleary-eyed, Mark entered Perth airport just after five in the morning. A carry-on bag was all he needed; he and Pat had already booked the red-eye return flight for the following morning. It would leave them both exhausted, and Thursday would likely be a total right-off. Luckily for Mark, Olivia would be in charge at Beaufort Gallery.

An exchange of text messages the previous evening had set up a meeting in Bellevue Hill for two p.m. with Greta, Sarah Green and the lead Major Crime investigator, DI Luke Brand. Mark still felt dissatisfied, even though his intuition had proven right that Angie's depiction of a painting by Horace Brodzky pointed to the close connection Brodzky had to Rachel Blazov. This had led directly to the initial suspicion that Brad Green had been involved in Angie's murder. So far, however, his input had been followed by three deaths, two of them completely innocent people. Moreover, the criminals responsible for these murders and, almost certainly, complicit in Angie's murder, remained at large while Greta and Lisa—and possibly other people—were still at risk of violent retribution.

Pat joined him in the departure lounge. "I'm not looking forward to these flights. They play blue bloody murder with my back." He eased himself into the seat next to Mark. "What do you think we'll find?"

"Don't know, Pat. The more I think about it, the more I wonder what Sam Green's options were. I mean, if he left evidence that exposed these criminals, that proof would simultaneously expose his own son as a murderer, and himself as a willing party to the cover-up. What would the point have been descending to such depths in the process of saving his son only to then throw Brad—and himself—under the bus by keeping evidence of the deal?"

"That's a fair point. But something makes me think that he will have retained a record of events. Not because he wanted to convict these people but so that, at the end of the day, there was a true account of what had taken place. His version of events, for the sake of posterity. That's what I'm looking for Mark. Not something Sam Green wanted *us* to find, but something he wanted future generations of his family to know. The truth."

The call to board their flight came, and the two men raised themselves slowly to their feet and joined the queue.

*****

"I'll be going to ground once this is done, Ray. For a while. I hope it's worth it for you."

"At my age, Danny, this is going to give me more pleasure than I'm likely to experience for the rest of my life. It'll be worth every cent I give you and every favour I owe you going forward just to deny that smart-arse bitch the satisfaction of investigating me. She hasn't got a hope in hell of pinning this on me. She won't find a thing. But I broke that old Jew and now I'm going to get rid of this dyke."

"I'm tailing her now. You'll hear about it when it happens."

*****

The taxi pulled up on Bulkara Road, Mark delighting in the curves of the tree-lined streets and the elevated position of the homes. He'd even caught a glimpse of the Harbour Bridge in the distance.

Two cars were parked on the opposite side of the road outside number eighty-three. He recognised Greta waiting at the front gate, slighter than he had imagined, with a solidly built man next to her he took to be Detective Inspector Brand. They paid for the ride, exited the taxi and crossed the road. The four of them exchanged greetings and Mark appreciated an immediate warmth with Greta. The vulnerability that he'd sensed during their conversation the previous afternoon seemed to have passed.

Inside the house, Mark and Pat cast their eyes to the walls. In the entrance area, there was an Impressionist era work of Sydney Harbour by Ina Gregory on one wall and a misty Melbourne street-scene by Clarice Beckett opposite. The two gallerists caught each other's eye and smiled. Hopefully, they'd have time and permission to look around the house at their leisure.

Entering the study was a strange, dream-like experience for Mark Lewis. He felt simultaneously excited and appalled, familiar and unsettled. To his left, inspecting the portrait he knew to be by Louis Kahan, was a short, squat woman. She turned to face them, her dark hair cut close, her pretty face disguising her age. "Hi. I'm Sarah Green," her voice crisp and clear as she approached them.

"I am so sorry for your loss," said Mark as they shook hands. Pat followed suit adding a small bow of his head.

"Thank you. It's been an awful forty-eight hours. I hope you can find something that helps us. I've been through the whole house and haven't found a thing."

Luke Brand summarised for them how they'd found the study. Every drawer had been opened and emptied, books and files pulled onto the floor, paintings removed and replaced haphazardly. Mark saw Greta's eyebrows lift at that description and he recalled her account of the unevenly placed painting that had led her to locate the Brodzky. If there'd ever been any USB sticks, Luke continued, they'd almost certainly been taken by the people who'd ransacked the study.

"Have you seen any of the hard copy documentation of the artworks?" asked Mark.

"There's files and files of stuff," said Sarah. "I've been through some of it but haven't found anything that helps."

"Well, we'd better start looking at it. Do you know which bits are which?"

Mark and Sarah moved towards the desk, and she lifted files off the floor and from the shelves, placing them on the desk. Mark sat at the desk and opened a manila folder containing old receipts from galleries whose names he'd only ever read about – Komon, Savill, Breuer, Wagner, Nodrum and more.

Pat had moved towards the Sam Leach and inspected it from close range. "Sarah? Do you recall a little painting that used to hang here? Before the Leach?"

"Yes. A little painting by Horace Brodzky. That was a gift to dad from my great aunt Rachel. It was dad's favourite painting. Or that's what I'd always thought."

"Do you know what happened to it?"

Mark wasn't sure if he should speak up, to let Sarah know they knew *The Masked Ball* was now in the home of the same person who'd ordered the murder of her brother and mother. He could see that Greta, too, was fidgety and uncomfortable.

"I wasn't really around here much back then," Sarah said. "For quite a long time actually. When I finally got my shit together, enough to let mum and dad help me, the Brodzky had been moved. I didn't ask him about it. Or mum. I got the feeling they didn't want to discuss it. But it's definitely not in this house. Or in dad's office. I've been there plenty of times. It might be in storage somewhere."

"Was the woman in that painting your great aunt?" asked Mark, unable to resist.

"No, definitely not. Aunty Rachel was short and round." She smiled, unashamed of their physical resemblance. "Dad knew all about her and Horace, and he had the details of the people in the painting written down somewhere. But I don't think the woman in the painting was ever meant to look like my great aunt."

Mark was visibly deflated, his theory toppled.

"What do you know about this painting?" Pat asked, pointing at the Leach. "Was there a particular reason he hung it in here, amongst these other works?"

"I don't know. It was here when I came back home. I think dad really liked it. He only bought works he loved. He especially loved smaller works, ones you could just pick up and walk out with in your hands. Just wrap up and take with you if you had to travel somewhere in a hurry. This one's more recent than the others, but I think it sort of pays homage to an older style of painting. Maybe that's what appealed to him. Or maybe he wanted to head in a different direction, as a collector?"

"I've got the paperwork for that Leach here," Mark said. "Bought from Sullivan and Strumpf in 2010 even though it was created in 2007. It's called "Lambda Butterfly". That explains the Greek symbol in the lower left of the painting. I suspect it hadn't sold at the original exhibition."

"Or it had been brought back by the initial buyer looking to cash in on a rise in Leach's prices," added Pat.

"But the point is that it was first hung here no earlier than 2010." Mark looked at Greta and she nodded her understanding. Sarah flipped through pages of a ring binder file, Mark sensing her discomfort and distraction at the discussion. The events of 2010 would likely be very new to her.

"Sarah, are we allowed to move these paintings?" Pat asked. "Take them down and see what's on the back?"

Mark could tell that Pat had become preoccupied with the butterfly painting. He turned to Sarah who had turned to Luke.

"Is it OK, DI Brand?" Sarah asked.

"I'm not sure we've dusted them for prints but looking at them now, I think we should have. But if you're wearing gloves, that should be OK." He withdrew some purple disposable gloves from his pocket and handed them to Pat.

Pat slipped on the gloves and removed the Leach from where it hung. Two wall screws about ten centimetres apart had been holding it up. The wall behind it was otherwise untouched. Mark observed with admiration and nostalgia the tenderness with which Pat handled the painting. His movements were adept and conveyed his sense of respect—almost parental love—for every work of art he handled. Fond memories of his first contact with Helen and Pat flashed across Mark's mind.

Pat stood the painting on the low table in front of a comfortable leather lounge, its broad, flat frame allowing it to remain upright without support. He sat down on the lounge and inspected the reverse side. Sarah was also drawn towards the Leach and stood behind the lounge, also examining the back board. It was made of sturdy black cardboard but was completely blank. Apart from single line that read:

"SamLeach_LambdaButterfly2007"

"Nothing to see," she said.

Pat continued to stare at the board. "That won't be the signature."

"I've found something here about the Brodzky," said Mark sitting at the desk. "There's a photocopy of *The Masked Ball* and there's a card ..." as he reached into the plastic pocket and withdrew a thin, worn envelope containing a cardboard gift card. On the front of the envelope was written "To Sammy". Mark withdrew the gift card with care, an image of a painting of two children on the front and, on the reverse of the card, attribution to the National Gallery of Victoria's collection; Russell Drysdale's "Two girls, 1945-6". Bought way back then, presumably from the NGA's gallery shop, Mark imagined.

Inside the card was a short note in elegant handwriting:

To my darling Sammy

Wishing you all the best on your Bar Mitzvah. I hope all goes well for you and that you read your portion expertly.

I left this gift with your mother because I knew I'd be overseas on your big day. I hope it always reminds you of your Aunty Rachel. One day I'll introduce you to the artist and have him explain the painting to you in person.

Meanwhile, all my love, you precious boy.

xxxxxxx

Mark exhaled. Under what sort of pressure had Sam Green been placed to allow this exquisite gift to be taken from his possession? Sadness mixed with rage welled up inside him. Greta came to look at the card which Mark, lost in a fog of melancholy, passed to her. Sarah too was drawn to the card, a testament to her great aunt who'd died when she was only five, and who Brad had never really met.

"Am I allowed to remove this backing board?" asked Pat, seemingly unmoved by Mark's discovery of what was, in its own way, a time capsule of mid-twentieth century Australian art history. Only Luke Brand seemed to notice the question and he looked at Sarah. Distracted, she looked back at him, processing what she'd heard Pat ask but to which she'd not really paid attention.

"Yes," she said as the question registered. "Just be careful."

"And keep your gloves on," added Luke.

Pat smiled and asked for a suitable implement, settling for the paper knife Sarah had retrieved from the desk drawer. He gently worked the knife under the board, lifting it millimetre by millimetre around its edges, careful not to tear it or damage the underlying frame. "The fact that there's no signature on this board tells me it's been attached later. The artist will have signed the work on the reverse side for sure."

Mark wondered to whom Pat was talking, struggling to comprehend his intense focus on this one painting. Barely conscious of doing so, Mark pushed back his chair and stood up, lured towards his colleague and *Lambda Butterfly*, all attention directed at its reverse side. They all gathered behind the lounge, looking over Pat's shoulders, something about his deliberate manner raising expectations of an important discovery.

Pat separated the cardboard and lifted it away, setting it down with great care next to the painting on the low table. The exposed back of the painting bore a sticker identifying the gallery and its Paddington address. The gallery must have since moved to Zetland, Mark noted. In black text it was signed "Sam Leach". There was no other writing at all, and no date, nor anything else to identify it or explain how it had come to replace the Brodzky.

Pat felt gently along the inner edges of the frame, his head tilted slightly to one side and his eyes creased in apparent disbelief. Mark was the first to move away, stepping back to the study desk to continue his examination of the various documents, unsure what Pat had hoped to detect but feeling dispirited nevertheless. Sarah and Luke stood up and moved away; Sarah offered them all some tea.

Pat was motionless, as if lost in thought. Greta alone remained behind him.

"Pat. Have a look at that backing board. It isn't lying perfectly flat. What's on the inside?"

Instinctively, Pat pressed down on one edge of the board, confirming that it rocked a little, its' under-surface not totally flat. He picked the board up by its edges and flipped it over. Stuck with clear masking tape to the centre of the board was a small metal object. Pat did not immediately recognise it.

"That's a USB memory chip," said Greta. She turned towards Mark at the desk. "I think we might have found what we've been looking for."

The room went silent. Pat slumped back in the lounge and reached for his lower back, Mark sensing a mixture of discomfort and satisfaction in his expression.

"How do we access what's inside it?" asked Sarah.

"Greta and I will have to take that for analysis," said Luke moving to claim the tiny piece of evidence, his movements now exuding a distinct sense of purpose. "Our IT people will be able to open it up."

"Take the whole backing board too. That looks like a password on the flipside," added Greta.

Luke nodded his head in acknowledgement.

Mark caught Pat's eye with a quizzical expression, in search of an explanation from his mentor, trying to comprehend his line of thought.

"It was the odd one out, Mark," said Pat. "He was trying to point us in the right direction."

Mark shook his head, perplexed but impressed. "Let's complete the review of all this paperwork, as well," he said. "I don't fancy having to fly all the way here and back in one day too many more times."

In the space of a minute, the mood in the Green's study had turned around, the sense of having been soundly thwarted replaced by one of distinct optimism. The plan was agreed, Luke offering to drive straight back to police headquarters with the chip and the backing board, Greta happy to stay and supervise the others.

As soon as Luke had left, Mark asked Sarah, "Can we have a look around the house?"

*****

Greta texted Lisa: *"Looks like we might have found something. An incredible story. Might have some guests for dinner. We'll go out. How was work?"*

"Well done. Hope it's over. Can't wait to hear. Work's been great."

Greta went over to the study desk and sat down. She recalled the expression of outrage Angie had painted on her own face and pondered the thread of connections that had led her to this moment. She made a mental note to call Aresh on the way home. The ringing of her phone interrupted her train of thought, but the name of Susan Lieb caught her attention and quickened her pulse.

"Hi Susan. Is everything OK?"

"Yes Greta. It's all fine here. But some heavily tattooed men on motorbikes just came to your front door and knocked. They tried to get in although not very hard. I was watching them from my front window."

"Did anyone come to check on them?"

"Yes, some other men came up to your front door within a matter of seconds. I couldn't really tell much about them. They all seemed to be chatting to one another. It looked a little tense, to be honest. The bikies made a big show of looking around the place, like they were planning to come back. Then they just swaggered off back to their bikes and drove off. I watched the other men and they returned to a car parked a little way up Midelton Road. I think they must have been colleagues of yours, probably just doing their job."

"Yes, I'd say that was just the bikies trying to let me know they're watching me. Did you see any particular emblem they were wearing?"

"Nothing I'd recognise, but I took a photograph through the window. You might recognise something."

"Thanks. Send it through as soon as you can. When did all this happen, Susan?"

"They only left about five minutes ago, no longer."

"Thanks Susan, you're an angel. You're as good as having the police watch my house."

"Greta," and Susan paused for a second. "I don't know how to say this. There was something a bit staged about all of it. I mean, what do I know about bikies?"

Greta could imagine Susan's facial expression, her trademark smile, at once self-effacing and knowing. Susan continued.

"It's just that something about it made me feel uncomfortable. As if they wanted your colleagues to believe that they were focusing on your home. It felt to me like it was a sort of diversion, when they're really planning to get to you somewhere else. When you're not expecting it. It's a ... just a woman's intuition. Please be careful, my sweet girl."

Greta thanked Susan again, pondering her advice, as another incoming call took her attention. It was Luke, calling from his car.

"Bikies have just visited your Bondi home. Nothing sinister, Gret, they were just pissing on your tree as far as we can tell. The guys watching your house were onto them quickly. Just trying to ruffle your feathers, nothing more."

"Did the guys figure out which gang they're from?"

"No. We didn't recognise the men they sent, and they weren't wearing any emblems. Just some stupid cartons to mock us. They're all fuckwits, Greta, you know that."

"Yes, but they're dangerous fuckwits, Luke."

"When we get this chip opened, Gret, I reckon we'll have Chalmers stitched. And the bikies will slide back into their burrows."

"Thanks for letting me know. Just get it looked at today, OK? I've got a bad feeling."

"I'm only ten minutes away from HQ. I'll get this done tonight if I have to."

Greta put her phone down on a small table in the entrance hall. She thought about her conversation with Susan Lieb. A woman's intuition? More like a protective mother's warning. She shook her head. She'd better call Lisa straight away. The call did not go through, so she sent a text:

"Just being careful but can you get an Uber back to my place and leave your car at work? Not sure it's safe enough yet."

Don't get in your bloody car, Lise, Greta thought.

Greta went out onto Bulkara Road. It was a fine day, cloudless but crisp. She scanned the streetscape for anything untoward, but all appeared peaceful. She knelt down on the verge and peered under her vehicle. Nothing seemed to have been attached. She walked around onto the road and repeated the manoeuvre. Nothing. She checked for any signs the boot or the bonnet had been forced. There weren't any. Then the doors. They all appeared undisturbed but still Greta was nervous and didn't try to open anything.

She could neither get into her car nor leave it on the roadside, in case someone else tried to open it and was injured. Or not, of course. The bomb squad was in Zetland and that was only fifteen minutes away by car. She didn't know what to do. She was panicked by Susan Lieb's concern, and by Ray Chalmers' vindictive nature. But calling out the bomb squad was never done lightly. And this seemed marginal even to Greta.

A fellow Academy graduate had been based there for years. They hadn't been close at the Academy, and she wasn't sure he was still working there. She closed her eyes and tried to settle herself; she rang the main switchboard and asked for Rowan Barber. He answered within seconds.

"Detective Barber speaking. How can I help?"

"Hi Rowan, it's Greta McCartney. I really need a favour."

"Oh yes. McCartney." Greta could hear his mental cogs turning. "You're the talk of the town, grassing out colleagues to bed a podcaster. Couldn't make it in Major Crime, so they've got you sorting out stealing as a servant. Why am I not surprised?"

Greta's was simultaneously offended and enraged. Her emotional reserves had been exhausted and something inside her snapped. "What a charmer, Rowan. You haven't changed one bit. But there's a bomb in my car that's been planted by one of those not-so-charming colleagues you refer to, and if it isn't deactivated before it explodes, I'll make sure this warning call to you goes viral. And you'll be the one checking on parking fines for the rest of *your* miserable career. If you're lucky." She didn't wait for a response but spoke faster and louder. "This is Sergeant Greta McCartney advising Detective Rowan Barber that there's a bomb in a car located at 83 Bulkara Road in Bellevue Hill." Greta checked her watch. "It is fifteen forty-three and I estimate it will take you no more than fifteen minutes to get here. Expected arrival of the bomb squad around fifteen fifty-eight." And Greta hung up the call.

Greta was shaking with indignation and fury. What a total arsehole, she thought. The whole lot of them. They could all rot in hell. She knew that she was fixated on the improbable presence of a bomb, but she really couldn't give a shit anymore. They could laugh her out of the Force, and it wouldn't matter. It was, she realised, a moment of total clarity. They could all just go fuck themselves. Miserable, small-minded, mean-spirited, puffed-up, moronic ... fuckers. She sat on the kerb, her elbows resting on her knees, her head hanging low, dejected, deflated. "Fuck you all," she muttered.

"You look like you're carrying the weight of the world." It was Mark. She hadn't heard him approaching. She stood up and turned towards him, his smile gentle and inquiring.

Greta shook her head but said nothing, dipping her chin to her chest as tears welled up in her eyes. Mark approached and put his arms around her. Thoughts of her father, who she hadn't hugged in twenty years, overcame her and she wept. Mark said nothing but maintained a firm hold on her, as if reassuring her that he wouldn't let her go. How odd, Greta thought, that, within a matter of minutes, two strangers would respond to her as if they were her parents.

Thoughts of Susan Lieb brought her back to the present with a start. "I'll try to explain," she sniffed, "but can we step away from the car? I've called the bomb squad. I think they might've planted an explosive device."

"In your car? When?" They walked about twenty metres from the car.

"Mark, this criminal bastard has bikie links. The bikies have been doing all this killing at his direction. And they've been around at my place today, trying to scare me. And I suppose it's worked. I'm a mess."

"Is everything OK with you and Lisa?"

"Yes." There were more tears. Trying to laugh through them, Greta said, "She's fine, we're fine. We're better than fine. It's just that I've been battling ... things for so long. Honestly. I'm done. Emotionally, I mean. I've been seriously on edge for forty-eight hours. I haven't slept. I hate my job. My family ... oh shit ... I've been so bloody ... alone for so long."

Mark put his arms gently around her again. In a hushed voice he said "You seem to be very good at your job. But you also seem to want to do it all on your own. It's a good thing to ask for help every now and then."

"Yes, but this *isn't* my job. I was kicked out of Major Crime by total ..."

"Arseholes?" Mark added.

"Utter shits who didn't want me to progress. And I was good." She stopped and pulled away, retrieving a tissue from her pocket and blowing her nose. "And I did ask for help today, from the bomb squad, and the moron I spoke to was so cocky and condescending. He barely knows me. He was just so comfortable belittling me …" She couldn't finish the sentence.

"But he agreed to come, didn't he?"

"I didn't really give him a choice. The truth is, there probably isn't a bomb, and when he proves that there isn't, he'll make my life miserable in every corner of the force. And revel in it. I'll be finished."

"And if there is a bomb?"

"He'll be the … the hero. You can bet on that. He's a bloody simpleton, Mark, I know this guy. *And* he's earning more than me. It's all just … total shit."

"Do you not want to stay in the police?"

"No. Not what I'm doing now. But I wanted to make it work. I wanted to prove that I could. That I was … as good as everyone else. Normal." She looked at Mark searching for even a flicker of judgement but seeing only concern. "I've somehow managed to stuff up almost everything I've ever done."

"Until this case." He smiled. "And Lisa."

"But three people are dead, and we still haven't arrested the culprits. I don't think we'll ever get the bikies. Look. Mark. I am crazy about Lisa, but I feel like I've been leaving a trail of ruin in my wake my whole life."

"And she's crazy about you, I guess."

Greta stepped back and Mark released her. She nodded. "Incredibly, she is."

Greta's phone rang and she saw that it was Lisa. She smiled, more at the thought of speaking to her girlfriend than at the coincidence of a call from her at that moment. "Hi darling, you got my message. I'm sorry to scare you."

"I'm getting used to these sorts of warnings from you. And experience has taught me that they're generally best followed to the letter."

Greta could imagine Lisa's mischievous grin in the sound of her voice. "I've had a real panic here and I've gone and called the bomb squad to my car which is parked in Bellevue Hill, outside the Green's house. I was worried about your car too. I mean, I'm still worried really. But I think I've overreacted this time." Greta tried to slow down aware that she was rushing her words. "They've taken that evidence we found in the house in for analysis. It looks really promising. If

I can just manage not to get you and me killed in the next twenty-four hours, I think it'll all be over."

Sirens in the near distance announced the imminent arrival of the bomb squad. Greta said goodbye to Lisa and watched as the lead police car arrived and the lead officer emerged, adjusting his collar. Greta moved to approach Rowan Barber, but Mark held her back by her arm. She glanced at Mark, confused, and he whispered, "Let him walk to you. I want him to know that I'm listening to every word he utters."

Rowan Barber walked up to Greta, looking uncomfortable at Mark's presence. "Can we have a chat?" gesturing to Greta to move away for a conversation in private.

"This is Doctor Mark Lewis from Perth," said Greta, holding her ground. "He has been assisting New South Wales police in our search of the Green household. This is my car," she said pointing behind her and to her right. "I have reason to believe that an explosive device has been planted, possibly in the bonnet or the boot."

Barber appeared to consider his words. Again, he looked at Mark, then nodded, saying nothing at all and turning quickly and gesturing to his team which vehicle they needed to examine. As the team approached, Barber spoke to Greta and Mark. "Time to go inside … you two."

Greta called out a grateful warning to the swarm of colleagues descending on her car and she walked with Mark back into the Green household. In the entrance hall she turned to Mark. "Thank you. That was incredible. How did that work?"

"He's a bully, that's all. And he hasn't got the balls to insult or belittle you while someone else is listening. You made a smart call to use my professional title. You know I haven't practised medicine for ages."

"I'm not sure if I'm having the worst twenty-four hours of my life or the best." Greta put her hands up, palms towards Mark as if surrendering. "I'm going to cry again if I don't shut up." And Mark moved forward and hugged her once again. Greta cried, the anger and fear draining out of her with each gentle sob, like a tired child losing the battle to stay awake.

"Mark, you've got to have a look upstairs. You two – cut that out." It was Pat, more animated than Greta had previously heard him. "There's a 1950s Juniper up there. I can't believe it. I remember this work from when it sold in Perth more than forty years ago. I had no idea it had come to this collection. I'm sorry to interrupt your cuddle, but you won't be coming back here any time soon, Mark, so you've got to take it all in while you can."

Greta could sense that Mark had been reprimanded and she gently pushed him away. "Go look at the paintings. I'll have a sit in the lounge."

Mark headed off up the stairs with Pat. At that moment, there was a distinct change in the level of energy in the voices of the people outside. There were some louder cries, then counter-cries. Greta could tell something was happening out on the road. Rowan Barber appeared at the door, flustered, and quickly spotted Greta. "McCartney. We've found a bomb. It's a small tilt-fuse device placed close to the petrol tank. A vibration trigger most likely. We're going to need a bit of help. You … stay in here until I've given you the all-clear." And he turned on his heels and went back out onto Bulkara Road.

No acknowledgement that she'd been right after all. No "thanks this is going to make me a hero". Greta didn't mind. A pervasive calm swept over her, and she slid deeper into the lounge chair, nestling its comfortable fabric. A large painting of flowers adorned the wall in front of her. She had no idea who'd painted it, but she was happy to absorb its beauty and joy in ignorance. From where she sat, she could also keep an eye out for Mark and Pat, so they didn't wander out onto the road. She shook her head as if hoping it might help her make sense of the day's events. Then she phoned Lisa.

Chapter 29
Thursday, 15 June 2023

Rowan Barber had been much less reluctant to have his unit check out Lisa's car, which had been left parked, unobtrusively, in her office carpark. His team was as relieved as Lisa that there was no bomb to be found.

And, on Greta's request, a media announcement was issued that a car bomb directed at a member of the New South Wales police force had been detected and deactivated by bomb squad personnel, pointing to a person of interest in the recent spate of gangland killings in Sydney. That was intended primarily as a message to the bikies to indicate to them that Ray Chalmers would soon be linked to the violence and that it was time for them to stand down. How Chalmers would respond to the broadcast of that information was unknowable.

Greta had waited up until two in the morning hoping for some news about the chip but eventually caved in to her exhaustion and to the effects of the wine she and Lisa had shared with Mark, Pat and Sarah over dinner. She was woken at seven by a call from Luke Brand.

"Whoa! You sound as if you've been out celebrating. Sorry to have woken you up."

"Celebrating for sure – and waiting up 'til all hours for you to call. What've you been doing?"

"I've hardly slept a wink, either."

"Sorry, Luke. I get it. What've you got?"

"It's incredible. It was password blocked, you know, and that was the correct password on the back of the painting. That's another point for you, McCartney."

"Thanks, Luke. But we'd never have even considered what it meant if Pat O'Beirne hadn't persisted with that butterfly painting. I have no idea how these people think but thank God that's how they do."

"I reckon this has been a bit of a team effort, Greta." Luke paused briefly. "I want to apologise for how I treated you, and I don't just mean during this case. I'm as guilty as the others for … judging you. Unfairly." He paused again, and Greta waited.

"So, that chip is an audio recording of Sam Green. I've just checked with Sarah who confirms that it is her father's voice, but there's a Word file on the same chip of a signed affidavit by a Justice of the Peace that makes it clear that Sam Green made the recording of his own volition."

"Did the JP listen to the recording?"

"Definitely not. He just affirmed Green's claim of authorship of the contents. And when you listen to it, you'll understand why Green wouldn't have wanted to let anyone else hear it. He describes his involvement in the cover-up from the moment his son brought the problem to him. It turns out that Brad had been a bit of a lead foot and had found a way to buy some favours from policemen to keep his speeding offences off the record. Quite a few favours, it turns out. When he found himself in Angie Richards' studio flat, looking for a painting he was sure she'd made but he couldn't find, angry and coked up, he punched her. Just once, he told his father, but she was struck unconscious, fell backwards and hit her head on a concrete step. He waited half an hour to see if she roused but she was blue and lifeless by the time he called his police contact for help. That's how and when he was introduced to Ray Chalmers. You kinda know the rest."

"Does he talk about the painting. The one from his aunt?"

"He does, and that is the hardest thing to listen to. He goes into quite a lot of detail about his aunt, what he knew about her relationship with the artist, the fact that he'd had that painting in one or other of his rooms since he was thirteen years old. He gets quite emotional as he pours out his disdain for Chalmers, for insisting on including the painting in the deal. It's quite venomous. Honestly, Gret, if not for the painting, I don't think Green would have bothered with this audio recording. He'd have probably let it go. But that part of the deal was sort of the straw that broke his back. Broke his will. Who knows, if Chalmers had only taken the money, we probably wouldn't have a thing to pin him on. It was his greed that undid him."

"And his hateful nature," added Greta. "He's a merciless bastard. Have you got him?"

"Teams are heading to both of his residences as we speak. Provided he's at one of those places, we'll have him in hand this morning. He's done for. You did well."

"Please let me know when he's been located. Not that I ever want to see or speak to him again."

*****

Linda and Mark had invited Helen, Pat and Aresh over for dinner, an early start to take in the six o'clock news over a sombre drink. Earlier on, Greta had contacted Mark and Pat, leaving Lisa to call Aresh, to tell them what had transpired.

They gathered on comfortable chairs in front of the television, Aresh still a little distracted by the display of paintings covering the walls. Mark had wrapped Angie's painting and brought it home to give back to Aresh. Lisa had been clear that she didn't want it back.

"What do you think you'll do with it now?" Helen asked Aresh.

"I'll probably hang it back it in my study. I was drawn to it from the very start, you know, and I still am, despite the truth of its story."

"Or possibly because of that truth," added Mark. "Innocent people have died, for sure, but the crime it lays bare has been solved and its principal architect has been exposed."

Linda handed out glasses of champagne as six o'clock approached.

"Mark said that you got to see the Brodzky painting," said Aresh, looking at Pat. "What did you think?"

Pat smiled. "It's a gem. It's little wonder poor Angie Richards took such note of it."

"I get that, but don't you think Greta took a real risk by taking the painting home with her?"

"I'm sure she knew it was a risky thing to have done," Mark chimed in. "She only told us what she'd done after we'd all left Bellevue Hill, I suppose when she felt confident that Chalmers was going to be trapped. She'd broken the rules for sure. If Chalmers had gotten away with it, she'd have had to admit she'd misappropriated evidence."

"Or maybe she'd have just kept it to herself until that vindictive bastard was dead," said Helen. "She could have denied ever having seen it—hidden it if she had to—and returned it to Sarah Green when she knew it was safe."

"Maybe," said Mark. "Either way, I think Greta really understood why the painting was important to the Greens. Why it was important in its own right. I think she really gets it." Mark looked at each member of the group, knowing that they also understood the depth of the painting's worth, of the importance of both Brodzky's painting and Angie's.

"She told me she handed it back to Sarah this morning, as soon as the whole story became clear. I honestly don't know if Chalmers would have got rid of the painting, but I wouldn't have been the least bit surprised if he had. I really believe that Greta saved it."

The television news began, and they gave it their full attention.

In an early morning operation, New South Wales police raided the outer Sydney home of a retired former deputy police commissioner wanted for questioning about the recent spate of gangland killings in Sydney. Inside, the police discovered a body presumed to be that of the retired policeman.

Police Commissioner James Everett gave a brief press conference this afternoon:

"On entering the house at a property north of Mulgoa close to the Blue Mountains National Park, police found the body of a deceased male aged in his seventies. There were no suspicious circumstances. Alert levels in respect of the recent killings around Sydney have been downgraded. I have no further details at this stage".

Mark turned off the television as the next news story began. He turned to the group and raised his glass but could find no words. Each returned the gesture and took a sip.

Acknowledgments

Horace Brodzky was born in Melbourne in 1885. He was already recognised as a talented artist by the time he left Australia with his parents and all but one of his siblings in 1904. Thereafter, he lived and painted in New York and London, although he spent his last forty years almost exclusively in the Kilburn and Willesden suburbs of London. He never returned to Australia, and he never achieved the recognition or commercial success his considerable early artistic achievements would have suggested. He is largely unheralded in his country of birth but is undeniably a significant "brush stroke" on the broad canvas of twentieth century art in Europe, the USA and Australia.

The Masked Ball first came to Australia in the 1980s having been purchased in London by an Australian collector. Carolyn and I acquired it in 2001 through Pat and Ian Flanagan. The identities of the four characters it portrays were never, to the best of my knowledge, expounded by the artist but there is broad consensus that the character on the left is Horace; without doubt, he was inclined to portray himself in some of his paintings and he frequently included friends and family as incidental characters in his works.

Since Brodzky was inclined toward caricature as well as portraiture, the other characters depicted in *The Masked Ball* might well be likenesses of friends and associates rather than realistic reproductions. My personal view is that he has depicted his two, close artist-friends, Jules Pascin and Mark Gertler, both of whom were more famous as artists than Brodzky, both of whom committed suicide at their artistic prime, and both of whom were, along with Brodzky, Jewish. The identity of the central, unmasked female figure remains less certain but, I suspect, was based upon a model he had engaged for this and others of his paintings.

It is lasting testament to Brodzky's wit and intellect that, almost a century after this mysterious and beautiful work of art was painted, we are still puzzled about the identity of three of the four characters and about the meaning of their arrangement and their gestures. And that it is the identity of the unmasked character, in particular, about whom we are most uncertain.

In 1934, according to Henry Lew's lavishly illustrated biography of Horace Brodzky, Horace was visited in London by an Australian woman by the name of Ella Dunkel who was eighteen years his junior. It is clear that Ella and Horace became friends and lovers; he gifted her paintings, photographs, drawings and a linocut when she left London to return home to Melbourne, probably in late 1937 or early 1938. Ella travelled back to Europe in 1945, returned again briefly to Melbourne in 1948, and then headed back to Germany (she spoke German fluently) later that year. I have formed the view that she is depicted in a painting by Brodzky entitled *Reclining Figure* painted in 1952 which, if true, might place her back in London at that time.

Victorian electoral records make it clear that Ella was living in Melbourne in 1954. She was gifted another painting by Horace, made in 1959, entitled *Group of Four Figures*—one of whom I also believe is Ella—from which gift I think we can assume she was in London at that time to have received it if not, in addition, to have been depicted in it. Electoral records establish that she was once again living in Melbourne, this time for good, from about 1961.

Although Lew describes Ella as having been a physiotherapist, I can find no record of that fact. She is described in various reports as a kindergarten teacher and appears to have had a strong social conscience, working as a welfare officer and for the benefit of refugees when she was in Germany in the mid to late 1940s. She never married, had no known extended family, and bequeathed all eight works gifted to her by Horace (including *Group of Four Figures*) to the National Gallery of Victoria when she died in 1979. *The Masked Ball* was not, as far as I know, ever gifted to Ella Dunkel as is implied in this novel.

Needless to say, many of the aspects of the fictional Rachel Blazov in this story are built upon what I have been able to establish about Ella Dunkel. Rachel Blazov's father, born David Spira in Blazowa in Galicia, is a fictional descendant of the very real Rabbi Tzvi Elimelech Spira, at one time the Rebbe of Dinov, also in southern Poland. The Bluzhever sect of Chasidic Jewish life, which arose from the Spira dynasty, remains active in the USA today.

Almost all of the paintings and artists referred to in this story are real. Importantly, the exquisite *Lambda Butterfly*, by renowned Australian artist Sam Leach, exists in Carolyn's and my collection and is signed, verso, simply "Sam Leach" in black texta. We acquired it from Sydney gallery, Sullivan and Strumpf, when that gallery was situated in Paddington, prior to its move to its current location in Zetland.

A number of bona fide residential and business locations in greater Sydney and Perth are described in this story and all have been included in this work of fiction to provide a sense of reality. None of these locations has been the scene of any of the fictional events described; nor are they the residences or places of business of any of the characters (or sorts of characters) described in my story. I hope that the current owners and occupants, should they read this book, will appreciate the artifice to which their cafes, homes and buildings have contributed.

Huge thanks to the entire team at Austin Macauley Publishers and, in particular, to Sophie Randall, Vinh Tran and Luke Davies for their support and patience in bringing this work to fruition.

I am grateful to Henry Lew not only for his beautiful books about Horace, but for his generous assistance as I tried to better understand Horace Brodzky and *The Masked Ball* in particular, the existence of which Henry was well aware. All other characters named in this book are entirely fictional and any resemblance to real people, living or deceased, is coincidental.

I am indebted to Sarah Levitt for her expert editing; to Mick Grainger for his input into matters relating to the police force about which I knew almost nothing; and to Paul Levitt for his local knowledge of Sydney sites and roadways. To Joyce, Paula, Pat, Ian, Mark and Anna – my sincere thanks for providing their honest input into the earliest versions of the manuscript, which greatly enhanced the final product.

And to Carolyn, as always, my heartfelt gratitude, for more or less everything.